THE WORLD ENDS TONIGHT

THE EDWARD KING SERIES BOOK FIVE

RICK WOOD

BLOOD SPLATTER PRESS

ABOUT THE AUTHOR

Rick Wood is a British writer born in Cheltenham.

His love for writing came at an early age, as did his battle with mental health. After defeating his demons, he grew up and became a stand-up comedian, then a drama and English teacher, before giving it all up to become a full-time author.

He now lives in Cheltenham, where he divides his time between watching horror, reading horror, and writing horror.

ALSO BY RICK WOOD

The Sensitives:

Book One – The Sensitives

Book Two – My Exorcism Killed Me

Book Three – Close to Death

Book Four – Demon's Daughter

Book Five – Questions for the Devil

Book Six - Repent

Book Seven - The Resurgence

Book Eight - Until the End

Shutter House

Shutter House

Prequel Book One - This Book is Full of Bodies

Cia Rose:

Book One – After the Devil Has Won

Book Two – After the End Has Begun

Book Three - After the Living Have Lost

Book Four - After the Dead Have Decayed

Chronicles of the Infected

Book One – Zombie Attack

Book Two – Zombie Defence

Book Three – Zombie World

Standalones:

When Liberty Dies

I Do Not Belong

Death of the Honeymoon

Sean Mallon:

Book One – The Art of Murder

Book Two – Redemption of the Hopeless

The Edward King Series:

Book One – I Have the Sight

Book Two – Descendant of Hell

Book Three – An Exorcist Possessed

Book Four – Blood of Hope

Book Five – The World Ends Tonight

Non-Fiction

How to Write an Awesome Novel

Thrillers published as Ed Grace:

The Jay Sullivan Thriller Series

Assassin Down

Kill Them Quickly

The Bars That Hold Me

For Joshua, Joey, Millie and Elodie

I'll let you read them when you're old enough!

"Let not your heart be troubled; you believe in God, believe also in Me. In My Father's house are many mansions; if it were not so, I would have told you. I go to prepare a place for you. And if I go to prepare a place for you, I will come again and receive you to Myself; that where I am, there you may be also."

John 14:1-3

JUNE 2002

TWO YEARS, SIX MONTHS SINCE MILLENNIUM
NIGHT

CHAPTER ONE

*K*elly hesitated. She edged through the room, wandering aimlessly, her thoughts twisting and contorting into troubled questions. As she dawdled past Derek's ageing book collection she allowed her fingers to trace their dusty spines, leaving a finger trail amongst the dirt of Derek's library.

"Eddie really looks up to you, you know," she spoke, a soft absence in her voice.

"Well, I believe, someday," Derek replied, "we will all look up to him. He's destined for great things, as I am sure you realise."

She managed a feeble nod as her body slumped against a nearby desk. She folded her arms and huffed, unaware she looked so troubled. She grew lost in her heavy thoughts, her perplexed conundrum, glaring gormlessly at a faint coffee stain ingrained in the carpet.

"Why don't you tell me what is troubling you?" Derek said, stroking his neat beard inquisitively. He leant gently against the bookcase, making sure not to disturb his excellent collection of old and sacred texts.

1

"I don't know…" Kelly muttered with a vacant shake of her head. She glided to the books, gazing at them absently, then drifted to the window, her eye contact remaining free of Derek's.

"He thinks the world of you, you must know this," Derek assured her. "He would do anything for you."

"I know. And I believe that."

"So, what is it?"

"It's… night terrors."

"Is Eddie struggling to cope with your sleep issues?"

"Oh no, Eddie's brilliant. Out of everyone, he's the only one who has experienced first-hand what I went through. He knows how to help me."

"So, what's the problem?"

"It's Eddie's sleep. He's getting really bad night terrors, sometimes worse than mine. They are getting more and more frequent."

Derek paused. This threw him. It wasn't like Eddie to have night terrors; the last time Eddie had a sleeping problem was because he was being disturbed and troubled by the demon Lamashtu. In fact, these issues were what prompted Derek to meet Eddie. A chance encounter, though some could argue it was fate.

But Eddie had disposed of the evil entity latched onto his soul; Derek had made sure of that. Since then, Eddie had trained his mind to become calm, a sea of serenity, a resolute gathering of complicated thoughts that never seemed to trouble him. So it was strange for him to be having them now, especially as an exorcist at the top of his game.

Then again, Eddie had gone to Hell. To rescue Derek. And God knows how much trauma and insomnia Derek had suffered as a result of that experience.

Surely the ordeal had put a strain on Eddie's psyche just as much, even if he hadn't shown it.

"I'm going on a journey," Derek announced. "To find answers. To find out why Eddie has these powers; to find out more about these prophecies. Hopefully, when I return, I will have more knowledge to guide you."

"But what should I do in the meantime? He's so... vacant, sometimes."

Derek leant against the desk beside Kelly. Normally he would react strongly to anyone leaning on his desk, especially when there were organised papers that they may be obstructing.

But when it was about Eddie, it didn't matter.

"Have you spoken to him about this?" Derek asked.

"Briefly. I mean, not really. It's just tough when he spends so much time supporting me."

"Maybe you should try talking to him."

"He'd deny it. Tell me nothing's wrong."

"Maybe there isn't."

"But how could there not be, when he's going through this?"

Derek shifted uncomfortably, mulling over useless ideas, dwelling on trails of thought that led nowhere. He couldn't deny it — he didn't have the answers.

Everyone always looked to him for them. Expecting him to know what to do. But in all honesty, sometimes it just came down to lucky guesswork.

"What do you think I should do, Derek?"

Derek stood, pulling his tie up, tucking his shirt in and rearranging his suit jacket. Tidying himself up was an act Derek had come to recognise in himself as an avoidance technique. A way of distracting himself from having to deal with whatever was in front of him. He felt strongly about always appearing smart, but fidgeting with his clothes was a sure sign of his discomfort that anyone else would just pass off as his 'tidiness.'

He told himself to stop it.

He looked into Kelly's melancholy eyes. She was so young, so innocent. Derek couldn't have been happier for Eddie and Kelly as a couple; but there was no denying that she didn't have the experience Eddie had, and maybe that made it a struggle to cope.

Truth was that Eddie could deal with his night terrors and any issues that came his way better than Derek could, and better than Kelly could. Kelly needed the support, but Eddie... Eddie was something far more than they were.

"Eddie is the best man I know," Derek told her. "He is strong, and knows the difference between right and wrong more than any of us. Maybe talking isn't something Eddie necessarily needs to do."

She nodded, forcing a weak smile.

He was right.

Of course, he was right.

"Trust in Edward King. We owe him that much."

CHAPTER TWO

*B*andile had known, ever since that sweetly menacing little girl had visited his deathbed, that his decision on that fateful night would be his fatal undoing.

He had wrestled with the ifs and buts of his decision, entertaining notions of what it would mean if he had said no.

But that hadn't been an option. He had been young and selfish, and did not want to die.

If he'd have greeted death and denied the devil, maybe he would have been rewarded by a place in Heaven.

But he was young, foolish, and cowardly.

Though, if he was honest with himself, the only thing that had changed was that he was no longer young.

The devil had saved him from death and bestowed riches upon him. The devil had given him the gift of foresight, as selected though his prophecies were. He'd been given everything every man had ever dreamed of.

Unfortunately, it had come at a cost.

Just the idea of saying no to the devil was an impossible thought. He had to follow his duty. He had to follow the path set out for him by Hell. It was not something anyone could defy.

One does not simply contemplate facing the wrath of a creature made of pure evil.

Now there he was, part of The Devil's Three. Along with a disabled woman and a dead man, he had formed the triad that had called on the devil to restore the antichrist into its rightful body.

And they had succeeded.

Bandile was on his knees, in disbelief at what he was seeing. He was a big man, having had to work with his hands in hard labour to survive growing up in huts in South Africa, and had grown muscles that filled his black frame, giving him a lean, intimidating posture. But he found his lip quivering and his body trembling at the sight of what was happening.

Edward King, the man with a reputation as a noble exorcist with heartfelt intentions, was diving the sharp end of a knife into the throat of the girlfriend, Kelly – who had been captured by Bandile to be part of The Devil's Three ritual as 'the suffered.'

Eddie pulled the knife away and Bandile, along with all others in the room, watched intently with dropped jaw. Kelly's helpless eyes looked up at the man she loved as blood sprayed haphazardly from her neck and all over the room, fizzling out into a gushing puddle dripping along the floor.

Derek Lansdale, the man he had fooled so easily, watched on in shock, gasping.

"How could you…" His feeble eyes cried, crumbling as his body collapsed into an inconsolable heap on the floor.

"It was the only way…" Eddie whimpered.

Eddie's body stiffened, his joints contorting in various directions. His shed his skin like a snake's, peeling off and floating into ashes. His features moulded into a malevolent mess, red eyes looking over the room, claws and beastly features bursting out of him in a painful transformation.

Bandile glanced around the room. Two young women, supposedly friends of Eddie, backed up against the wall. Jason Aslan, who had been 'the dead' as part of the ritual, disappeared into floating pieces.

Eddie's skin was now dark and blood-red, with veins sticking out all over his body.

Bandile was not going to waste any more time in this room. He had done his part.

He turned toward the window that already had a few cracks tearing up its surface and leapt toward it, smashing through and leaving the disrupted living room, tumbling onto the painful bumps of a small hedge below.

He jumped forward and ran.

And he did not stop running.

He endured all the weather. From the beating of the furious sleet, to the frozen temperatures of night, to the harsh heat of the following day.

This continued for longer than he could tell. He had no home, and was scared to return to any places he'd once haunted, though he wasn't entirely sure why. He couldn't make sense of much in those early days, his mind awash with tormenting, chaotic thoughts shooting through his brain and exploding into fragments. He grew paranoid, anxious, even seeing things he wasn't entirely sure were there.

For days at a time all he would do was run, run, run. He would steal food, sleep under discarded newspaper in shop doors, beg for mercy from those who tried to rob him only to find he had nothing.

Then he ran some more.

Finally, he broke down. Collapsing on his knees in the middle of a busy town centre, he held his hand out for food, glaring with dizzy vision at the people who bustled past him. They all ignored him. He had nothing.

He stole. He fought. He wept.

He was a shattered wreck of a man.

His strong, muscular body deteriorated rapidly under the stress of his mind and the heavy strain upon his body. He starved, his dry throat parched, begging the devil for quenching that would never come.

He never once considered praying to God. He knew he would not be welcome there anymore.

The devil had offered him salvation. This was anything but.

His ribs became visible through his chest.

His bones ached.

He became accustomed to the headaches of dehydration, the emptiness in his stomach, and the pains in his chest, as he yearned for anything to sustain his miserable existence.

He longed for the devil to do something.

Bandile had done his bidding. Was he not coming to offer some salvation?

He knew he deserved no mercy, but he at least deserved a reward. A place in Hell, away from the torture, somewhere the devil could hold him high and rave about his triumphant contribution to the cause.

Then, one day, shivering in the doorway of a broken-down factory on a cold, lonesome night, he heard footsteps approaching.

He closed his eyes, hoping that whoever it was would leave him alone. Wished that they were not going beat him, or humiliate him, or mutilate him.

Then again, he decided, perhaps they would grant him the sweet release of death.

"Pafetick," one of them declared, in a screechy, anarchic voice. "Fort ee woz meant to be some big man?"

"Shut the fuck up," came a gruffer, more assertive voice.

Bandile felt the owner of the voice come down to his level, but he closed his eyes tighter, wishing to be left alone. "Oi, open yer fuckin' eyes."

Bandile did as he was told.

The owner of the first voice was stood, his head tilted to the side. He was topless, and unhealthily skinny. Every inch of his body was covered in tattoos, all of them either tribal, or scary laughing faces, or of the crucifix hanging upside down. A pattern of engrained ink ran along his lips, like the shadow of his teeth, adorning his face with ceremonial tattoos, even covering his eye lids and his ears with black patterns.

The other man, crouching down to Bandile with an arm rested on his shoulder, had a large beard. He wasn't as heavily tattooed, but still had his forehead marked with upside-down crucifixes and tears marked down his cheeks. He wore a long, brown coat that made him look homeless, and the hand that rested on Bandile was beneath a tatty, fingerless leather glove. Bandile noticed a swastika decorated his knuckles, and he immediately grew wary of a racist attack.

"Wh – what do you want?" Bandile begged.

The crouching man shook his head.

"My name is Dexter, and this behind me is Bagsy," he introduced with a rough, gruff, common voice containing a mixture of accents. "We've been waitin' f'you. Nah you're 'ere under a fuckin' doorway. What is going on?"

"I – I don't understand."

"'E sent us mate!" screeched the one called Bagsy. "We been waitin' for yous to lead us!"

"To lead you?" Bandile echoed.

"We worship him, in his name," Dexter explained. It took a few seconds for Bandile to realise they meant the devil.

Satan worshippers... Bandile thought to himself. *And they want me to lead them?*

"The antichrist has risen," Dexter continued. "The heir of Hell is here."

"Really?" Bandile responded, not knowing whether to be worried or pleased. He had seen it happen, but had since disbelieved his eyes.

"Yeah, an' we're worried 'bout these hoomans who fink they can do 'im in. They be raisin' an' army, or so we 'ear."

It took Bandile another few seconds to adjust to their voices and understand what they were saying. He assumed by 'humans' they meant Derek Lansdale, and assumed that by 'do them in' they meant... Well, to bring about a fatal end, or something to that effect.

"Okay," Bandile confirmed.

"So get up, you're comin' wiv us," Dexter told Bandile, grabbing him to his feet. "An' we ain't got no time to lose."

MARCH 2003

THREE YEARS, THREE MONTHS SINCE
MILLENNIUM NIGHT

CHAPTER THREE

*D*erek watched from the study window as the unsettled trees collided against each other in the frantic wind. The rain bashed against the house, a salvo of attacks against the window, beating against it like a broken drum.

He wanted to sleep.

More than anything, Derek wanted to sleep.

"And the reports are coming in this hour of more mysterious disappearances," came a voice over the radio Derek had forgotten he'd left playing. "Many of the world's greatest, most noble figures have vanished without a trace. In more than eighty reported cases across the world, law enforcement officers have said that there were no signs of struggle, and the world is yet to come to an explanation that satisfies all the conspiracy theorists that–"

Derek turned the radio off.

He glanced at himself in the reflection of the window and flinched at the bags beneath his bloodshot eyes. His collar was open, his tie hung three buttons down, and his shirt was half-untucked. He had never allowed himself to deteriorate to this state of scruffiness in his life.

But he had a meeting. He couldn't go to bed yet.

So he waited, watching the violent weather attack people running by, sending bins flying against the debris of a nearby field.

"Derek," came a well-spoken, elegant female voice from behind him.

He did not jump. He was expecting this.

The news report on the radio had left him in no doubt as to what was happening.

He turned around confidently, bestowing his eyes upon the most beautiful creature known to man. A faultless woman, with lusciously smooth black skin, long, black hair, and a white dress that glided off her curves as if by magic. Gabrielle was an angel through and through, there was no doubt about that. And, for someone who was thousands of years old, she did not show it.

"I suppose you've come for me, have you?" Derek prompted with an air of irritation in his voice.

"Yes," Gabrielle confirmed. "Are you ready?"

Derek turned back to the vile storm. The weather was no coincidence. The end was near and the environment was furiously retaliating; though most people would be gazing at the spring gale and thinking it was an ordinary storm, with no idea of the omen it was announcing.

The heir had risen. The devil would follow. And then the depths of Hell would be unleashed.

It made sense to go with her.

To be evacuated. To run. To save himself, along with the other people deemed good enough to rescue.

But Derek hadn't been one for making sense lately.

"I'm not going with you," Derek decided.

"Please, Derek, don't do this—"

"I'm not doing anything. I'm just not going with you." He stared absentmindedly out the window without turning back to her. "You can leave now."

She took a stride forward. He could feel her pained eyes reaching out to him, beseeching him. He had no doubt she understood his reasons, but she would still try and argue the contrary. It would do no good. Any attempt to persuade him would be futile.

"Please, Derek, you must come with us."

"What, go with you so I can watch everyone who isn't worthy enough die?"

"This was how it was always going to be! You read the books, you saw when the prophecies ended. The rapture is coming, and God is evacuating the worthy. And you have been honoured enough to be chosen as one of them. Please don't stay on Earth to die."

"I'm not staying on Earth to *die*."

"The apocalypse is coming, we can't stop that. There is nothing more Heaven can do. Surely you can understand this?"

"Then maybe Heaven isn't trying hard enough!" Derek screamed, hauling his entire body around until his heavy arms pointed in the direction of Gabrielle. He was suddenly panting. His heart punched against his chest as if bashing against a cage.

An uncomfortable silence followed where all that could be heard was Derek's heavy breathing. He was infuriated. Incensed.

"With all that we've done, all the fights we've entered, all the lives we've lost!" Derek spat. "And you are telling me that Heaven — that *your Holy One*, is just packing it in?"

"This isn't the first time something like that this happened, Derek."

"Oh, please."

"You think you're the only world out there with life on it? You think you're the only world where something evil has risen up and taken hold? We've done this many times. We've seen what it is like to fight it, and we have seen how pointless it is. We are not abandoning Earth, we are being rational."

"That's not what it feels like."

"Derek, please–"

"Just *go!*"

Derek's fists clenched, a surge of fury firing up and down his spine, his gut filling with hate like poison. He could see it dawning on Gabrielle's face. It was useless.

Derek was not going.

"This is your decision? You are just going to stay on Earth to die?"

"No, I am going to stay on Earth to fight. Dying is something that happens in life. Your God created life, and he created death, so surely he'll know that."

Gabrielle sighed and turned toward the door, pausing one last time.

"Are you sure you will not come with me?" she asked.

"God and heaven may have given up on earth," Derek said. "But I haven't."

With a flickering white light she was gone, leaving Derek to glare at the empty space where she had stood.

Suddenly, he felt very alone.

CHAPTER FOUR

*E*ternity begins with an earth-shattering moment.
The jolt of two eyelids shooting open.

The squint against blinding light. The flinch away from the vast luminosity encapsulating any mortal person's vision.

Eddie fell to his knees, producing a mouthful of bloody vomit, coughing it over the rough surface.

His stomach was in inscrutable pain, twisting and throbbing into bumps of harsh acid, churning his vacant insides like butter.

But there were no insides. He felt hollow, empty. But still heavy. Like he felt the weight of burden pinning him to the floor like dead weight.

Where am I? his mind weakly wondered.

He rotated his head, taking in his surroundings. The walls felt like they were closing in. He was boxed into a room that had barely a few yards between each wall. The walls themselves were made of large, dirty stones, fading from grey to dark grey. Against the walls was a subtle blue illumination, shading the walls with the colour of the ocean.

Beneath his bare feet was straw. Many pieces, covering a

bumpy rock surface. No matter where he walked his feet hurt, whether it was from the sharp spikes of straw or rough bumps of harsh gravel.

Noticing something on one of the stones in the wall, he stepped forward, surveying it intently.

They were scratch marks. Five definite corresponding lines where someone's nails had dug in and dragged. The more he looked, the more he noticed detail in the carvings. Words such as, "save me," "God help us," or, "no hope here," were carved at various points of the wall, only visible when Eddie was close to them, squinting against the dark light.

At first he went with his instinct, frantically scouring the walls for a weakness. There was no door. But maybe if he could find a weak stone, something he could move…

He went through every stone he could reach, pushing it, prodding it, grappling with it.

There was nothing. No escape whatsoever.

He looked upwards, peering into the sky above that just faded into darkness. He was no doubt in a pit, but if the pit had an opening, it was far out of his reach. The sturdy walls disappeared into the darkness above, narrowing into nothing but distant black.

He leapt up, pushing his fingers into the cracks between the stones, hoping he could somehow climb, manoeuvre his way upwards — but doing so sent a shockwave through his body and sent him firing on his back.

He groaned in anguish. It hurt.

Something about the stones was stopping him climbing. They were cursed somehow.

He'd been in Purgatory before. He'd been in Hell before. But he did not recognise this place.

And he was certain that it was not Heaven.

A shock fired through him, like something was inside his body, writhing like a wild creature. Every muscle in his body contorted, like his whole body was a tightened fist, pressing against itself.

He screamed, allowing the pain to escape his lips.

It did nothing.

It was still agony.

He struggled against it, fought against whatever was holding him still, whatever was holding him captive.

With a defiant shriek, he collapsed to the floor. He curled up into a ball, shaking, quivering, overwhelmingly alone. Terrified, but at the same time, hesitantly curious.

Where am I?

This was not his world.

This was not somewhere he belonged.

He dropped his head and closed his eyes, trying to will the migraine away. But the soreness of his cranium only grew greater, harder, his stolen mind beating against his fragile skull.

When he lifted his head up there was something there. Like a screen, but with fuzzier edges. In front of him, a blurred image.

He watched it intently as the image drew into focus.

It was Kelly.

Oh my God, Kelly.

The screen grew, wrapping around his face, and played out an image like it was through his eyes. Like he was the one committing these actions.

His hands held onto a knife.

His hands plunged it downwards, into Kelly's throat.

He watched as she cried out in pain, looking up into his eyes with a helpless lack of understanding.

The moment went into slow motion. He lived it again.

And again.

And again.

Just as he already had numerous times.

Watching that look in her eyes as he did it, as the person she loved and trusted most in the world betrayed her. Then she went limp. Flopped into a heavy body spread out upon the floor.

The final thing Kelly saw before she died was him killing her.

It all came back. It thwacked him like a punch in the gut.

The image changed. He felt his arms stiffen, grow, his nails elongate into claws, and within seconds he was a vast, snarling, carnivorous hellbeast.

Then he snapped out of it. He was back in the dark, dank dungeon, completely perplexed.

That's when he realised.

He wasn't Eddie.

He was, except not all of him.

This body he looked down at was not his own body. It was an image of his body. He could see it clearly, but it was not his body. It was his mind inventing what he needed to make this experience make sense.

He was merely a soul. The remains of what was.

Eddie was in Hell or on Earth. Rising up as the heir and slaughtering innocent people. Preparing for the devil's ascension. Getting ready for the rapture.

And this is what was left. That one piece of Eddie that was good.

His soul.

That thing that had to be used so he could be conceived by Hell.

Trapped.

If only I could get out, find a way back, I could put this piece of good back in my body, I could...

No.

It was useless.

There was nothing he could do.

He peered around himself. It was empty. Nothing but stone walls rising up into a dark abyss until there was nothing left.

There was no entrance. No exit. No way in or out.

Nothing he could visibly see.

He had no powers.

He wasn't Eddie, he was just a soul. His body had changed. His face had changed. He had no real hands he could pour spells out of. He had no way to fight.

He had to rely on his friends. Derek. Jenny. Lacy.

They could do it.

Surely, they could do it.

And the dawn of realisation struck his mind like lightning.

He was stuck in a cycle. Watching the pain of his loving girlfriend die again and again. Realising he could do nothing to stop it or save it. All because it was some part of a sick game.

Some part of Eddie's sick game.

The heir of Hell's sick game.

A way to keep him trapped. Keep him going crazy. A way to ensure his maddening state only worsened as he found no resolve that he could use to escape.

And it was working.

He had no idea how long he had been trapped there.

All he knew was that his body was being used as a vessel for hatred. An entity occupied it with malice and cruel intentions.

If there was a low point, he had far surpassed it.

He only hoped his friends would not have to suffer.

He knew Derek would try.

He knew Jenny would try.

His faith had to be put in them.

CHAPTER FIVE

*C*ircling a few fading ice cubes in a half-empty whisky glass, Derek sighed at the few drops of therapeutic booze he had left. The ice cubes collided with each other so ungracefully, just three little circles left crashing around in his tumbler.

He downed the rest of the glass, grabbed the whisky bottle from the side of the chair, and filled himself back up again.

He looked down. Open collar, loose tie, shirt untucked. A prickly beard like the wild hairs of an untamed animal.

It suddenly struck him what he had once said to Eddie.

"One must be presentable, whether you are meeting the mother or taking on the very depths of Hell itself."

Derek scoffed.

The irony.

So much said to guide a wayward man, such advice that he had now neglected.

Realising he was starting to pity himself again, he took another large swig of his whisky to numb his mind, relishing the sharp uncomfortable sting scalding the back of his throat.

He had never been one to wallow in self-pity before.

But his advice had never resulted in the death of so many before.

He was not the one who gave up, who wavered in their disbelief of others, who gave in and let a single crease of shirt be unfolded.

But recent events had debilitated him. They had gone some way to wearing down his resolve. This only incensed him further, knowing he was better than that, knowing that he wasn't a weak man.

He was everyone's rock.

Well, sometimes he got tired of being a rock.

Tired of training Eddie.

Guiding Martin.

Being Heaven's bitch in each and every one of their battles.

He retched at the thought of the glorious angel of Gabrielle being sent from his Almighty, with the intention to fetch him away from Earth. To remove him from a war he had been waging for years. Because he was supposedly special. Because he was worthy.

"Hah!" he grunted, and took another big gulp.

Worthy?

He shook his heavy head, dropping his pounding, drunken mind, and directing his absent gaze to the crumbs ingrained in his carpet.

How was he worthy?

He remembered the words he'd said to Martin. What he had told him.

They had lingered by the side of the field, waiting for Martin to decide whether or not the army should fight the heir.

Derek had declared that they would follow Martin.

Derek had believed in Martin.

Derek had known it was the right decision.

Turns out he had known nothing.

Now they were all dead. The army they had gathered, the

powerful, supernatural forces recruited from around the world. Dead. Slaughtered. Pulled apart by a demonic, genocidal maniac.

The world had lost the only people with the power to resist what was to come.

And all because he'd told Martin to keep going.

He had to be Martin's rock. Martin was inevitably inconsolable following the army's death. Following the loss of Jenny. But Derek couldn't let that cause him to falter.

There was too much resting on Martin's young shoulders to let him think he was to blame.

"It is not your fault," Derek had reassured him. "And you can't let it be your fault. Self-doubt is a bigger enemy than the heir; you need to believe in yourself."

Derek snorted.

What bullshit.

The only part of that Derek truly believed was that it wasn't Martin's fault.

Because it was his.

He had told Martin to make the decision. He had followed the call of a delinquent seventeen-year-old without thought or hesitation. Because he thought it was right.

Now look where they were.

He finished his whisky. Grimaced as he poured too much down his throat. Withdrew the bottle once more and filled himself up to the top. Stared at it. Circled it, watching the whisky temporarily stain the inside of the glass as it whipped around seamlessly.

He closed his eyes.

"Sorry, Jenny," he whispered.

He lifted his head back and chugged a large gulp of whisky down his sore throat. He relished the sting, relished the pain, relished something breaking this absent knowledge of what they needed to do.

"Sorry, Eddie," he whispered.

Glared at his glass.

Swilled it in another circular motion.

Downed it.

Filled his glass up.

Downed it.

Closed his eyes.

Tried to dream. Tried to think. Tried to rid his tired head of all the justified negativity.

After a few more glasses, he passed out.

CHAPTER SIX

*A*n crash into the bench sent broken shards of wood against the back wall of the house. The garden was a mess of splinters, with wooden wreckage lying across the grass like small pricks of failure.

Martin sighed. It wasn't working. He'd been at it for hours.

But if he was to become the heir's equal...

He must have a range of spells.

Fuck a range of spells. Cannot be arsed.

But he knew that, despite how assertively he may think that, he did not believe it.

It took hard work. Patience.

The only problem was that Martin had never been one for patience.

"Right, again," he demanded of himself.

He stuck his right hand out, spinning his finger in a small, circular motion. The faster he got, the more a spark ignited, a golden flash echoing his movement. As the flashes grew more frequent he increased the radius of the circle he was creating more and more, until he had created a circle of light that turned from flickers to a fully formed circular edge.

Watching carefully, ensuring he picked the exact correct time, he plunged an open palm forward. The circle flew across the garden and, for a moment, Martin was hopeful.

Half of the circled wrapped itself around the bench, then the other half ignited into a fiery mess, exploding planks of wood to shatters in the process.

"Argh!" Martin growled, turning his head to the sky and collapsing on the floor. "For fuck's sake!"

I've been at this for hours!

He had the basic spells down; conjuring elements, throwing fireballs, plunging a gust of wind into an opponent. But the last time he'd faced the heir, these spells had proven useless.

He had to learn something better.

He had to *be* better.

It was just so bloody difficult.

Martin huffed and lifted his head to glare at the remains of his attempts.

A restraint spell. Conjuring a circular edge out of condensed fire, throwing it forward, and trapping your opponent. If he could do this, he could temporarily hold the heir, then hit it with lethal attacks.

But who was he kidding?

The heir would not allow itself to be trapped in this shitty excuse for power.

Martin allowed his mind to wander and stumble upon memories of school. His so-called friend, Simon. Kristy, the girl he'd fancied more than anything.

He wondered what they would be up to now.

Simon would probably be down the park underage drinking or hanging around outside McDonald's, intimidating passers-by.

Kristy would most likely be getting off with whatever guy she let take her around the back alley of Primark.

Even so, Martin felt a pang of jealousy.

They were still living out their lives, exploring their youth, taking the time to discover who they were. If they did something dickish, it would be all right, because "they are just kids."

Such reasoning didn't apply to Martin.

Not anymore.

He couldn't be just a kid. He was only just approaching eighteen, but had a responsibility that no adult in this world could understand.

He dragged himself reluctantly back to his feet.

If at first you don't succeed...

Once more he rapidly rotated his arm, creating a circle, making the elements fit just right. Then once he had a perfect solid base of gold, he threw the circle forward, watching it crash into the bench and smash the final remains to oblivion.

...then scream and cry and tell everyone to fuck off.

What if this had never happened? What if he had never gone to Eddie about his mother? What if Cassy had never come to him and placed this burden on his shoulders?

What would he be doing?

Intimidating some old lady. Starting fights with anyone who gave him a dodgy look. Convincing himself that he didn't need stupid, pathetic school.

Yes, this was a horrible fate, but at least it stopped him from being a dysfunctional yob.

Oh, what he wouldn't give to be able to go back to ignorance... To deny that any of this was real, to return to his incessant prickishness, to continue hating everything and everyone. To be able to throw a teenage tantrum, kick off at a teacher, shout at everyone that it wasn't fair that he was being made to learn maturity.

He would never have had to witness death. He would never have had to see Father Douglas' demise, Jenny's body being ripped apart, or the violent end of the entire army they had gathered.

An army.

What a mistake.

This burden was his, and his alone. Derek was a huge support, but even so, ultimately, it was up to him.

Heaven conceived him.

No one else.

So he needed to get a grip.

Stop daydreaming ridiculous fantasies.

It was over.

That old life was over and he could never go back.

This was his life now.

Waiting to fight.

Waiting to die.

Or, just waiting.

"Fuck it."

He lifted his arm out and began the circular motion once more.

CHAPTER SEVEN

*E*ddie's mind spun with empty thoughts; absent ideas racing manically around his vacant mind.

He had no idea how long he had been lying there, but he knew that it was making him go crazy.

As he imagined the devil would be intending.

His back ached less, as if he was getting used to the uncomfortable bumps he laid upon. He didn't know what was worse; feeling the pain, or being there for so long he became accustomed to it.

What struck him most was the complete absence of anything. No stimulus, no interaction, nothing to do but sit and ruminate — it stirred his mind into a fever. If he wasn't careful, he was going to lose his sanity.

If he had sanity.

Does a soul have sanity?

Yet another thought that could swim around its mind until it drowned in the sea of unanswered questions.

A faint whirring attracted his attention. A small spinning from behind his head.

He sat up, opened his eyes, and peered at a small image unfolding before him.

Upon this screen was a field. The weather was torrential, rain beating furiously down upon the soggy grass.

But the lightning and the rumbles of thunder weren't what attracted his attention.

The screen was through the eyes of something. Of someone. And beneath these eyes were a mass of people, full of supernatural gifts, hurling different spells at him, conjuring vast amounts of elements, bombarding him with everything they had.

Before he had been able to muster an idea as to what this screen was, it had shot forward and wrapped itself around Eddie's eyes. Eddie could now see through the screen as if he was physically in it.

Because he was in it.

At least, part of him was.

His hand reached out, revealing a sharp claw, bigger than several human heads. Below this claw was a mass of puny humans, all of them fighting, attempting to oppose him.

He resisted anything they threw at him with tedious ease. His claw swung down in retaliation and swiped through several throats, splattering blood into the rain as the bodies turned limp.

This was him.

He was doing this.

He could feel it. Every swipe he took, he could feel the soft tissue of their throats ripping at the tip of his fingers. Thick, red blood seeped through his claws. The stench of death was overwhelming.

And the rage.

It soared through his body like a hundred volts of electricity, purging him of any positivity, soaking him until he was drenched with a detesting of everything.

It belonged to him. All of this belonged to him. This body, this anger, these raging thoughts — they were his.

Eddie ripped himself away from the scene that had wrapped itself so securely around his face, diving to the floor, doing all he could to tear himself away from the trance.

He lay on the blank floor shivering, covering his head to protect it from being consumed by this vision again.

He knew what it was.

He knew he was looking through the eyes of the heir of Hell. He knew he was slaughtering innocent people with the ease of slicing butter. He had no control. He was in there, feeling everything, but in the backseat; whatever was driving him was not of this world. It was something completely and entirely evil.

But how many did I kill?

As if something wanted to torture him with the answer, the screen changed. Eddie lifted his weak head, ignoring his painful migraine, and watched, allowing it to wrap around his vision once more.

It was done. Now it was a sunny day and the field was covered with bodies. A few of the corpses were intact, but most weren't; it was like a butcher's bin. Body parts, bloody heaps of unrecognisable limbs, dead rips of skin. Everything was unidentifiable. And he had done all of it.

Derek.

He saw Derek traipsing despondently through this field, looking around himself, recoiling at the horror.

So much death.

Derek couldn't see him.

Derek didn't know he was watching, hiding.

Derek paused, closing his eyes, dropping his head. Like looking at the suffering was too much. Like he couldn't bear to see it.

Like he couldn't bear to see what Eddie had done.

The man he had trained. The man he had nurtured, taught, watched evolve into a powerful soldier of good. Now the cause of so much pain and misery.

It was more than Eddie could take, and he was about to look away until he saw that Derek wasn't alone.

Someone was there. Someone bright. An elegant, white dress folding their body into beauty; long, blond hair, a beam of positivity.

She wasn't of the mortal world, Eddie could see that.

Then he realised. He knew who it was.

The girl who died when he was a child. The girl he had freed from Balam. The girl who had set all the terrible events of his life in motion.

"Cassy…"

Now a grown woman, except… she was more than that. Accepted by Heaven as a soldier for good.

Working with Derek.

Working with Derek in the fight against humanity.

Working with Derek, against Eddie, in the fight against humanity.

His heart stung. He collapsed to his knees, unable to control tears from escaping his eyes.

The little sister he had loved so much. He'd lost her as a child. He had fought to save her. He'd battled for her soul, to have it freed from Hell.

Now she was taking the last stand against the brother who had done everything for her.

Because she knew it was right. Because she knew that it was what this Eddie would want her to do.

And he did want her to.

He wanted her to make him stop.

"No more…" he whimpered, wanting to go back to the monotonous absence he had been suffering. To return to the tormenting, vacant room so he didn't have to watch those he loved weeping over the mess he had made.

Anything but this.

Anything to relieve this pain.

But he could not escape it. Everywhere he turned, her torment was decorated over his vision. Her face as she cried at the anguish caused by him.

"Cassy, it wasn't me!" he said, wishing she could hear her.

Her head rose. A flicker.

As if she was reacting.

As if she had heard something.

"Cassy? Can you hear me?"

She froze. Her eyes widened. Something was taking hold of her.

"Cassy!" he cried out with everything he had, his vocal cords straining under the pressure of his scream. "Free me! I'm trapped, I'm here!"

The image disappeared. As if someone could see what was happening.

The sounds, the feelings, the smells. It all went. Eddie was back to the dungeon again.

He didn't know if she had heard him.

But it was worth a fraction of hope.

CHAPTER EIGHT

*T*he field was stained with the remnants of loyal fighters. Everywhere Derek looked he saw death, torture, and mayhem. He tried to raise a mental barrier to it, conceal his emotions, put a block on his emotions.

But it was tough.

It was so, so tough.

Walking amongst the remains was unbearable. He'd had the call that morning that the church was sending people to conceal it, to cover it up. To make sure no one went near it. The authorities had been paid enough to keep the public away, and Derek expected them any moment.

But part of him wished they didn't arrive.

So what if everyone saw this? Surely people should know what was coming, and what they were up against.

If only to ensure that they knew the devil was real, and that he was coming — so very, very imminently.

"Hi," came a soft, feminine voice from behind Derek. He didn't need to turn around to know who it was. He remained dawdling, stepping over a mangled bloody lung, between a contorted leg, until it was too much. He had to look up to the sky, if only to stop looking at the destruction spread across the field.

"Do you know what I don't get?" Derek began, turning to Cassy, her angelic state shining over the darkness of the field. "Is why your stupid God allows this to happen."

"It is unethical to mess with free will."

"Unethical?" Derek exploded. "You're talking to me about what is unethical? Standing by and watching people fight in His name when He could bloody do something is ruddy unethical!"

"Derek–"

"And then your stupid head angel comes down with plans to evacuate when all of you could come down and fight and rid us of this damn mess!"

"Derek, calm down," Cassy said, not raising her voice one bit. She placed a reassuring hand on Derek's back, watching his face tear with emotions he couldn't handle. "This isn't you."

"I have been here for years, doing His work, and I have said nothing. I have called on Him to remove demons from innocent people's bodies. Why do I need to do that? Why do I need to call on Him to do this, when He could so easily do it Himself?"

"But he has fought back, Derek. He gave the world you. And Martin. And sent me to guide you. That is him playing his part, and it is quite a stretch as to what he could do without messing with free will."

Derek shook his head, turning his angry eyes to Cassy's elegant gaze.

"It's such a cop-out."

"Derek, please don't let this get the better of you. You've been a strong and stable leader. For all of us. Myself included. You need to keep the faith."

"Keep the faith?" Derek echoed, disdain in his voice.

"You've got to–"

Cassy's eyes grew wide and she grasped her chest as if she'd just taken a heavy punch in the gut.

"Cassy?"

She fell to her knees, her eyes practically bursting out their sockets, reaching out a helpless hand. Derek rushed to her side, placing a hand on her back, trying to steady her, but the pain was evidently vast.

As she scrunched her face and her body up, battling the agony, she moaned an exasperated wail.

Then she froze. She uttered a quivering gasp, her lips shaking, her eyes open wide.

"Oh, dear God," she gulped. "Eddie…"

Derek's brow furrowed. He kept his arms around her, steadying her, with a longing need to know what she was seeing.

"Cassy," she spoke, in a voice slightly altered, as if it was deeper; it was her speaking, but with a different tone entirely. "It wasn't me."

She choked. Closed her eyes. Then opened her mouth once more.

"Cassy, can you hear me?" she spoke in the same man's voice.

She fell to the floor, rolling around, groaning, then froze once more. Her eyes shot open.

"Free me! I'm trapped, I'm here!"

Derek recognised that voice.

But no…

It can't be…

Then, with a final flourish of her fluttering eyelids, Cassy fell flat out on the floor, her body no longer tense.

"Cassy," Derek said, kneeling beside her. "Cassy, are you okay?"

She shook her head. "It's Eddie…"

She reached her hands out and used Derek's body to help her clamber to her knees.

"What about Eddie?"

She ignored him. Instead, she pushed herself onto her feet and aimlessly wandered away, unconsciously stepping over various entrails. Her hand rested on her forehead, her eyes scrunching together as if dealing with a horrific headache.

"Cassy, please," Derek said, walking after her. Whatever she had seen, he needed to know.

If it was to do with Eddie, he needed to know.

"It's Eddie," she tried to explain, stumbling over her words. "But not Eddie…"

"What does that mean?"

"It was Eddie's soul, I'm sure of it."

"His soul?"

Cassy turned to Derek, fixing her eyes on his.

"He – he's there."

"There? Where's there? Where is he? Is he going to do something else? Is he going to kill more people?"

"No, it's… not the heir of Hell. It is Eddie."

"But Eddie *is* the heir of Hell, Cassy."

"No." She shook her head. "His soul still remains good. I've seen it."

JANUARY 2000

MILLENNIUM NIGHT

CHAPTER NINE

"*T*hat the best you got?" Eddie taunted the demon before him with a cocky grin.

Balam rose out of Adeline's body, hovering in the air. Its three heads — that of a human, a bull, and a ram — each snarled and snapped at Eddie. Its human head lifted its frown into an aggressive growl, its bull head snorting readily, and its ram head beat against its own chest in desperation to kill this bastard.

It had been a tiresome exorcism on the night of the new millennium, and Eddie was growing weary. But he knew that, now he had ridded Adeline's body of Balam, he could save Cassy from Hell. There was no doubt Balam had Cassy's soul, captured for torture, kept in Hell for what Balam must intend to be an eternity.

Eddie was determined to do this. Determined to save her from this prince of Hell's evil clutches.

He would die before he gave in.

Balam growled again. This time not to intimidate, but to show aggressive displeasure at being well-matched. Eddie had already ridded young Adeline's body of Balam's possession and, for this reason, it felt increasingly weary. It had struggled to defeat Eddie and was giving its last attempt at fighting by throwing a series of flames forward.

Eddie lifted his arms in a swiping motion and forced the flames to cease, to drop to the floor in a handful of ash. He threw his arms in the air, exploding a ball of wind before him, forcing Balam to thwack against the far wall, dropping to the floor pathetically.

"Free my sister!" demanded Eddie, a scream filled with rage and resolve.

He rose his arms, forcing Balam into mid-air, rotating and rotating its body, faster and faster, until the ram screamed, the bull helplessly snorted, and the human face begged for mercy.

"Free my sister!"

Balam's body bashed against the wall, again and again. This would be too much humiliation for this proud prince of Hell to take, and Eddie hoped this would be enough to open Balam's clutches and to take Cassy's soul back.

"I command you, bitch of Hell. Release her!"

Balam screamed out, its voice getting caught on the wind of its spin. The room was a tornado of chaos, objects turning to weapons against Balam as they were caught in the middle of the whirlwind it created.

Eddie chuckled as the ram head squealed in agony, enjoying seeing this thing suffer.

"It is done!" Balam cried out.

The body of Cassy rose out of his muscular, scarred chest, rising into the centre of the room.

Balam did not stick around to see the two reunited, and neither would he want to. With a fit of aggression, his body instantly sank downwards into the ground. The room disappeared as it plummeted and plummeted, further and further, until it found itself slamming its aching back against a large stone, back in the pit of Hell.

It lifted itself off.

It was livid.

Fought. Defeated.

Embarrassed that he'd had to free his servant.

Back in Hell to let the devil know that he had let Heaven's child go. That he had been defeated by Hell's own creation. That the prince of Hell was not worthy of its king.

The chains Cassy had been kept in lay absently without an owner across the rocky cliff. Balam had enjoyed torturing many souls across an eternity of human civilisation, but never had enjoyed torturing a human spirit the way Cassy's had been tortured — after all, this was the daughter of Heaven. Heaven's conception, forced to face an eternity of pain.

Now, nothing.

Balam's pride was severely wounded. A huge dent in the ongoing belief that he was better than anyone, or anything. Especially those peasants on earth.

Now he had been defeated by Hell's child.

He swore then and there that he would have revenge. When they brought out the heir of Hell, when it rained fire upon the weak earth, Balam would rise. He would find this Cassy girl and reclaim her.

There, Balam would continue to torment her. To wriggle inside her until he made her bleed, to slash her with a thousand continuous flicks of a sharp whip, to rip her in two and feed on her insides then watch as they agonisingly grew back. To humiliate her, to rape her, to watch as she squealed under his three heaving heads.

When the time was right, Balam would return to earth.

Balam would march on up to Heaven and snatch her out if he needed to.

Cassy would face an eternity of his rage and torment.

And at that point, Edward King would have fulfilled his true destiny, and there would be no way to stop him.

MARCH 2003

THREE YEARS, THREE MONTHS SINCE
MILLENNIUM NIGHT

CHAPTER TEN

*M*artin watched with his mouth agape as Derek and Cassy frantically paced the study, musing over possibilities that were completely nonsensical to him.

"It could be a trick."

"It could be fake."

"Or it could be real."

"What if there was a way to reach him?"

"Could we bring him back?"

"Would he come back right?"

"Would it matter?"

"Of course it would."

"Are you sure what you saw was real?"

"The devil couldn't play a trick on an angel, you're not mortal."

"It must be genuine."

"It must be real."

Eventually, Martin sighed, growing frustrated, and tried to interject.

"Guys?" he offered.

"Where was he?"

"I have no idea."

"Guys?" he tried again.

"But why now?"

"Where has he been all this time?"

"*Guys!*"

They both froze, turning their muddled stares toward him.

"What the hell is going on?" he asked, waving his hands in the air.

Derek and Cassy sat, realising they needed to calm their ideas and fill Martin in. Slowly but particularly, Derek explained what had happened in the field.

"What do you think it is?" Martin mused. "I mean, are we sure it's Eddie?"

"If it was something you or I saw," Derek answered, "then no, I could not be sure. However, I am certain Hell could not interfere with a servant of Heaven so easily. If they could, the angels would be entirely wiped out by now."

Martin nodded, trying to make sense of what Derek was saying.

Had she really seen Eddie?

Because Martin had battled this thing and it was nothing like the Eddie he had briefly met — it was evil. Eddie had turned into it — not just metaphorically; Eddie had literally changed into a demonic beast. Derek had witnessed Eddie physically transform after the ritual of The Devil's Three, then disappear to Hell. Eddie had become this thing.

So how could he still be out there when his body wasn't?

Martin had faced it. Just after Jenny had appealed to the Eddie within; and if anyone could appeal to the Eddie within, it would have been her.

So where had the true Eddie been then?

The thing had slaughtered everyone they had gathered for an army. All the most powerful experts in the fields of the paranormal and supernatural had been wiped out within minutes.

Eddie wouldn't do that.

Unless this wasn't Eddie they were dealing with. That piece of the devil within him could have taken over, pushing Eddie to the background. Could he really still be in there? Could he really be stuck, watching everything the heir of Hell was doing, helpless to stop it?

After all, the body and soul cannot exist without each other. Maybe Hell had to bury Eddie somewhere deep down so they could keep the heir.

"Right. Well, what does this mean then?" Martin asked, realising he had been in silent thought for a while.

"I think it means we have a chance of bringing him back — the true Eddie, that is," Cassy answered. "Maybe that is the only way to defeat the heir. He's too powerful for any of us to kill, so maybe we have to beseech the Eddie within."

With an infuriated sigh, Derek stood from the table and turned away, vigorously shaking his head.

"Derek, mate, surely you see Cassy's right?"

"It's not that," he grunted, refusing to turn around.

"Then what?"

He leant against the bookcase, loosening his collar, dropping his head.

"It's Jenny," he answered.

Martin shot a confused glance at Cassy.

"What about her?"

Derek took a deep inwards breath, then let it go slowly. He turned back toward them, doing all he could to gather himself, to retain some composure.

"It's just — oh, God… I've been a fool."

Martin shrugged at him, prompting him to explain.

"If I'd have only listened to Jenny," Derek said, "then maybe… She was so adamant Eddie could be saved, and I wasn't having any of it. If only I'd have listened, she'd still be alive." He closed his eyes and hung his head. "They'd all still be alive."

Martin looked to Cassy, hoping she would have something reassuring to say, but she didn't. At first, Martin wasn't inclined to argue either, instead agreeing with Derek that they should have listened.

Then he remembered all Derek had done. Not just for him, but for their fight.

"You made the call you had to make," Martin reassured him. "You made the decision with the info you had, and I dunno if I'd have done differently."

"He's right," Cassy said. "None of us had any idea. You can't beat yourself up over it."

Derek absently nodded.

Martin knew Derek knew they were right. But he also knew that it would not stop Derek from beating himself up or doubting himself. It must be tough to constantly be the strong one, and to put this decision entirely on his shoulders wasn't right.

Martin only wished there was some way he could let Derek know that.

Martin decided that a change of conversation would help.

"Right. What do we do now?" he asked. "With us knowing this, what do we do?"

Derek turned to the window and looked out at the vast horizon, the setting sun in the amber evening sky.

Derek shrugged. "I have no idea."

CHAPTER ELEVEN

There could be no doubt about it – he had seen them.
Derek and Cassy.

Alive.

How could Eddie reach them?

Laying in a sinisterly dark room, lit with a hazy blue tint, with nothing but his ruminations and incessant thoughts to accompany him, it was a question he lingered on for a while.

Maybe if he tried, just closed his eyes, and really tried, he could get through to someone.

Jenny would be his best bet. He was closest to her, they grew up together; they could practically read each other's minds already. What's more, he knew that out of all of them, she would be the one who could recognise him trying to make contact.

She would never give up on him, he knew that.

So he knelt, closing his eyes and concentrating, ignoring the bumpy floor digging into his knees.

He concentrated the way he would when conjuring an element, preparing for a fight, readying himself for an exorcism.

He listened to the absence. Smelt a distant linger of smoke. Felt his movement against the stone walls.

Everything melded into one piece of nothingness.

He just had to think. Had to reach out. Had to hope that she would hear him.

Jenny.

I'm talking to you, Jenny.

He pictured her face.

Her long hair, her infectious smile. Lacy by her side, holding her hand, always loyal.

Jenny frantically searching for a way to get Eddie back.

Eddie knew that's what she would be doing.

He looked for her in her home. Thought about her making a cup of tea, or sitting on the sofa watching a movie with Lacy.

But he couldn't see her there.

A vague outline of Lacy appeared, but no Jenny.

So he tried harder.

He could not fail.

He had to get through to her.

Jenny, can you hear me?

Nothing.

Maybe if I spoke it...

"Jenny, please, can you hear me?"

He waited.

"Jenny, this is Eddie. It is actually me. But I need to know you can hear me. Come on, please..."

He waited.

And waited and waited.

He didn't know what he was waiting for, but he knew he'd know it when he had it.

He had such great powers, such a gift; if anyone could do this, it would be him.

Surely.

"Jenny, come on, I know you're there, do you hear me?"

He felt nothing.

"I'm alive, Jenny. I'm here, but I need your help."

He listened intently.

Really straining himself to hear any sound, any feeling, any smells or touches that reminded him of her.

Something. Like the graze of her hand against his. Like the sound of her voice in the distance of his mind. Like the look in her eyes when she saw he was upset.

But all he had were his desperate thoughts, continually and unsuccessfully reaching out for her.

All he could feel was a longing, blank space.

"Come on, Jenny."

No.

It was useless. Futile. Pointless.

He collapsed onto his back.

It was no good.

He was stuck there.

CHAPTER TWELVE

*T*he devil's throne spiralled lavishly into the air away from the spewing lava and choking ash of Hell. He sat upon it, casually poised upon a gigantic set of skulls that allowed him to look over all the eternities of suffering and torment.

Watching over the demons enjoying their torture of various souls made him giddy. Like a child unwrapping a birthday present, excited to see what was in store. Loyal demons swarmed the surroundings, unleashing terrific tirades of torture over every inhabitant trapped in a world of volcanic sorrow.

One of his most trusted demons approached, slithering toward him on the endless serpent tail that attached itself to its muscular torso. Its dragon wings were thrice the size of its body, with sharp claws fixed to their end. Each of its three human heads had a body that attached itself to its slithering lower parts, each with horns pointing triumphantly into the air of ash. Along its body were sharp spikes that could slice an enemy in half before it even knew what was happening.

The devil had seen it. Humans had been decapitated before they had even laid eyes on this monster.

It was magic. Brilliant beauty decorated in bloody bunting.

What was more prominent than the sinister movement and ferocity in its eyes was the immense evil it exuded. To be in the presence of this demon was like being in the presence of pure hatred, something the devil drank like water.

"You called for me?" spoke the demon, Geryon.

"Yes. And you came."

The devil smiled, watching his loyal servant a moment longer, enjoying the detestable, exuberant hostility encircling Geryon's face.

"What can I do for you, my Lord?" Geryon requested.

"The soul of Edward King, the living good of the heir we cannot kill," he began. "It's trapped. But it's finding ways to reach out."

Geryon nodded, listening intently and obediently.

"He has even tried to reach out to his friend, Jenny." The devil burst into hysterics. "But she's dead!"

He practically fell off his throne, such was the extremity of the hilarity he found in the situation.

The soul of Edward King was just so… pathetic.

Trying to reach out to the one person he couldn't because he had already killed her!

It was a beautiful kind of irony.

Geryon did not falter in its expression. It remained dementedly serious, patiently awaiting further instructions, a permanent grimace tattooed to its cheeks.

"What would you like me to do with him?"

"You are the guardian of Hell, Geryon," the devil answered, still cackling. "Guard him."

"As you wish."

"He cannot escape. You keep the door shut. Do not let him pass. Do not let him send messages or signals of any kind."

"Yes, my master. It is done."

Geryon turned and slithered away, its large claws clicking against each other with a looming tick. Its huge dragon wings flapped grandly, taking the demon into the air and on its path.

The devil sat back in its throne.

"You think it stands a chance of escaping?" came the familiar voice of the heir of Hell approaching from behind him. The devil could detect a tone of worry in the heir's voice, a longing not to let the soul out of his cage.

"No," answered the devil. "But time is of the essence. Enough waiting. Ready yourself. We are going to open the gates of the underworld and finally claim Earth for our own."

"Very good."

"My heir, my son — we are going to unleash Hell."

CHAPTER THIRTEEN

*S*ettling the chewed pen down on the table, Derek decided he needed to stop being so agitated. He wasn't himself. Whatever dreadful, terrible, fatal mistakes he had made, he needed to be calm and collected; even if just for Martin's sake.

He looked at the young boy beside him.

Not even an adult yet.

Such expectation weighed upon him. Quite literally, the weight of the world. The boy was supposed to be humanity's last salvation. He was Heaven's hand in this disaster, their roll of the dice. It was he who would fix this.

If he could.

Martin wasn't destined to do this, he had only been given the powers. There was nothing guaranteed he would even make a difference.

There was no prophecy about this. In fact, all prophecy books Derek knew of ended in the coming months. No one could predict anything beyond that.

Which could be incontrovertible evidence that this is where it ends.

But Derek couldn't accept that.

Then, suddenly, with a little spark of light tingling in his brain, an idea grew. A radical, ridiculous idea, but an idea nonetheless.

"How is your restraint spell coming along?" Derek suddenly inquired, suppressing a smile caused by the impromptu attack of his idea.

Martin sat back and shrugged, rubbing his eyes. He was evidently tired. In fairness to him, before all of this he had never worked a day in his life. He had walked out on school and refused to do anything. But the way he had dedicated himself to his role in all of this was nothing short of heroic.

Derek only hoped Martin realised that.

"Dunno, man," Martin muttered, shaking his head. "It's… not, really. It's more of a throw a circle and clatter the bench. Not really getting the hang of it."

"You will."

Martin scoffed.

"Oh, trust me, you can scoff all you want. You will."

"Yeah, what do you know?" he grunted, turning his head away. He was slouched, his hand resting on an anxiously bouncing knee, his face curled up into a scowl.

"Not much," Derek admitted, watching Martin intently. "But enough."

Martin went to reply, then thought better of it, instead choosing to let out a big sigh.

Derek recognised the teenager in him. Even saw a bit of himself at that age — the need to argue and defy anyone who tried to oppose his sceptical mind. However much was expected of him, Martin was still young, and this was how kids his age would react. With a tantrum; if that's what one could call it.

And Derek couldn't blame Martin if he was starting to lose

faith in him. Derek had been wrong a few too many times, and too much death had occurred as a result.

Derek abruptly stood, placing his hands on his hips. He meandered over to a cupboard, opened it, and withdrew a whisky bottle with two tumblers. He poured them and handed one to Martin.

"What's this?"

"Whisky."

"I've never had it before."

"Then today will be your first. Just sip it."

Martin took the glass from Derek, watching as Derek took a very slight sip from his glass. Martin took a swig from his and reacted with a repulsed face, completely disgusted.

"That's why I said sip it," Derek pointed out jokingly.

"Why are you giving this to me?"

"Because we are going to make a toast."

"A toast? To what?"

Derek hesitated. He peered at Martin. So young, so boisterous. He was like Eddie when Derek had first met him — completely unaware of what he was capable of.

"What do you reckon we should toast to?" Derek mused.

"There's nothing. We have nothing."

"No, that's not true." Derek shook his head. "We have the trees outside. We have the air in our lungs, for now. We have each other. We have the knowledge, you have powers, we have a life of memories, some happy, some sad. We have plenty we could toast. Just pick one."

Martin defiantly placed the glass on the table and shook his head.

"I can't believe you're trying to be positive after all–"

"My belief in God came *after* I had proof; before then, I was a passionate atheist, as I believe one should be until they see a reason to be otherwise. I hated how people believed in God because it gave them comfort. Why should you need God?

Look around you at this world, this wonderful life, these wonderful things. There is always so much to be thankful for."

Martin stared at his feet, mulling something over in his mind.

"No, we don't need a God. We need what we have. So, tell me, Martin – what should we toast to?"

Martin shrugged, then lifted his glass. "To Eddie, I guess."

Derek smiled.

"To Eddie."

They took another sip, and Derek couldn't help but be amused by another disgusted expression on Martin's face.

It was time.

Derek had to announce his plan.

"I'm going to perform an exorcism."

"You what?" Martin answered, full of confusion.

Derek sat beside to him, placing his glass on the desk, facing his prodigy straight-on.

"I am going to perform an exorcism on the heir."

"What?" Martin yelped, shaking his head with disbelief at yet another ridiculous, doomed-to-fail plan from Derek. "How the fuck are we going to do that? In case you ain't noticed, the heir ain't easy to pin down!"

"That's where you come in. And your restraint spell."

"Derek, I ain't able to do that restraint spell, it's shit!"

"Then make it not shit."

"I don't know what you are on, mate, but this is the most ridiculous plan I've heard yet."

"No. It's not. It's what I've overlooked. It's a possibility I never entertained and, however improbable or preposterous an idea it seems, it's the best one we have. We can't kill it. How could we kill it? But if, like Cassy saw, Eddie's soul is there somewhere, we need to access it. Bring it back. And the only way to do that is with an exorcism."

Martin stood, running his hands through his hair.

"This is just another plan to get us all killed."

"This isn't some ruse to get us killed, Martin, but yes, that is a bloody strong possibility!" Derek retorted, rising to his feet, doing his best to avoid becoming frustrated.

Martin looked back, seeing in Derek's eyes that he meant it. That he was absolutely determined to go through with it.

"I think you're a nutcase."

"Maybe," Derek replied honestly. "But it's time we had faith in Eddie. If I'd have done so earlier, Jenny may still be alive."

Martin didn't reply. He was torn. Torn between whether to go along with this or not. Despite being so nonsensical, part of it made sense.

"Yes, Martin. It is time to have faith in Eddie. Have faith that we can get to that part of him that is still good."

"And if we can't? If we don't manage to finish this exorcism and he kills us?"

Derek shrugged. "Then we won't be any different than if we did nothing."

CHAPTER FOURTEEN

*A*s a tear glistened in the corner of her eye she knew it wouldn't matter. She wished she was home, in her mother's arms, even in her neglectful father's arms.

But she had already felt herself becoming resolved to death.

Maybe on that first night, things had been different. She had remained optimistic of being found, or even freed. She had begged her captors and they had even given her hope.

It felt foolish now.

Kicking and screaming had done nothing.

If anything, it had only spurred them on more.

And, watching as they stood grinning at her, she knew the end was near.

And she was grateful for it.

After all the deprivation of water, the sexual humiliation, the cries of "we gots ourselves a virgin to offer!" night after night after night, the daily torture, the further loss of hope as every passing day went by — she felt ready for the sweet release.

She hoped her mother found her body.

That way it could give her a way to move on. A way to

ensure she did not keep hoping against hope that she would return.

"It's time," declared the one she had assumed was the leader. He was a large black man the other two often referred to as Boss, but had also been referred to as 'Bandile.' "Let's make the sacrifice now so the heir can grow stronger."

"But the more she suffers, the more strength she'll give…" spoke the one next to him with a large beard. She'd heard them call him Dexter.

The one they called Bagsy stood to the side of Bandile. Watching her intently. His sadistic eyes not blinking. He didn't appear to listen to a word the others said — he just kept chewing her up and spitting her out with his eyes. Those eyes made her stomach churn. Those eyes were the eyes she saw right before anything awful was about to happen.

"The one Heaven has conceived," continued Bandile, "is being kept in the home of Derek Lansdale. We know where he is."

Dexter turned his head with a sudden gasp toward Bandile, child-like excitement adorning his face with a wide, creepy smile.

"You lie!"

"I do not lie. We will kill him tonight."

Dexter's eyes refocussed on her.

"And this one?"

Bandile shrugged. "Finish her already. I got bigger stuff to do."

Bandile turned and strode out the room, Dexter following — giving Bagsy an approving nod as he did.

Bagsy, not removing his playful eyes from her for a second, tiptoed toward the door and locked it.

"Juz yoo an' me!" he sang out, the tattoos of his face creasing under his repulsive acne. He looked sickeningly unhealthy. Every time she had seen him he had worn nothing but grey shorts, revealing his heavily inked flesh. Satanic symbols and intimidating skulls mixed with snakes, grinning sinister faces and tears dropping from his eyes, marking his entire body with tattoos designed to put the fear of God in you.

Except, this man was clearly not a man of God.

He was from something else.

He crept toward her, his joints seeming to point in every direction as he moved, like an insect about to eat its prey. He moved to within inches of her face and she could feel his toxic breath wiping over her, fluttering her hair back as he let out a long, sickening exhale over her eyes, which she shut tightly.

"Do not close yous eyes to meez," he whispered in a voice that went up and down in pitch with such a lack of harmonisation that it became chaotic. "My love, we haz too much to do."

"Please…" she whispered. "Just kill me."

He reached his arms around her in an embrace that felt like she was being wrapped in barbed wire. He cut her rope open with a knife, allowed her binding to drop to the ground, setting her free.

She gasped.

"Are you… are you letting me go?" she asked, feeling a sudden rush of optimism.

With a slow nod accompanied by the sound of clicking bones within his contorting neck, she turned and looked around herself for an escape.

He raised an arm and pointed a thin finger toward a far door.

She sprinted forward, stumbling with eagerness.

She was going to see her mother.

Once more she would be reunited.

She could see her tearful face now; she could practically smell her perfume, feel her arms around her.

She dove at the door, clamped her hands around the handle, and pulled it.

It was locked.

She turned.

Bagsy stood directly behind her. She hadn't even heard him move. A low, sinister chuckle trickled past his infected lips.

"Please…" she begged, feeling that sudden rush of hope falling away.

In a foul swipe, he swept his knife forward and stuck it inside of her, sinking it into her ovaries.

She felt the knife tear up her, ripping through her belly and up to her chest. Everything dropped.

She could hear the wet thump of her insides dropping to the floor.

The last thing she saw before her dead head hit the ground was the wide grin of Bagsy's face as he revelled at her torment.

NOVEMBER 1999

ONE MONTH UNTIL MILLENNIUM NIGHT

CHAPTER FIFTEEN

*S*hards of glass smashed through the window and floated along the gust of wind. Manic screams and wails of all pitches consumed the room — every single one of them coming from the same young boy's body.

"I command you demon, be gone!" screamed Eddie, his youthful energy surpassing Derek's. Eddie's mentor stood at the side of the room, shielding his face from the large pieces of furniture firing around the room.

Eddie made a mental note to remove loose items from the room before his next exorcism.

"From all sin Lord, from your wrath, from sudden and unprovided death, from the snares of the devil I beg you to clutch this servant of God away from this wretched villain!"

The boy screamed as his body rose into the air, his bare, torn chest rising slowly toward the ceiling. Only a loose set of rags covered the child's dignity, revealing deep wounds and ravenous cuts up and down his legs and torso.

"From all lewdness, from lightning and tempest, from the scourge of earthquakes, from plague, famine, and war, save us from everlasting death and defeat this demon, oh Lord!"

The boy's head lifted, its demented eyes completely black, its sweaty hair entwined with dried blood and ectoplasm.

Eddie looked over his shoulder at Derek.

Derek had taken part in nearly a hundred exorcisms. This was Eddie's twelfth.

Yet there was a feeling of inherent experience in Eddie that he had somehow surpassed his guide. Derek stood out of the way, protecting himself from the chaos of the room, whilst Eddie embraced it. He took it on, willing the demon to do its worst.

"By the mystery of your holy incarnation, by your coming, by your birth, with the holy baptism of fire, free this child from this demon's clutches."

The flying objects of the room, the soaring glass, child's toys, ripped clothes — all of it froze. Poised in the air with a sudden pause. The boy's body hovered momentarily, then thudded back down to the bed.

This was it.

This was nearly it.

The boy's head lifted, directing its fiery stare at the boy's saviour. Eddie looked back just as intently, not withdrawing his glare, refusing to be the one who gave in.

"By your cross and passion," Eddie spoke, this time in a calmer voice, enunciating every syllable like he was spitting bullets. "By your death and burial, by your holy resurrection, your wondrous ascension, the Spirit, the Advocate, on the day of judgement — please, Lord. Please. Deliver this child from evil."

"You may think you have won," the demon choked in a deep, croaked whisper. "But you fight for the God you defy."

Eddie stepped forward, presenting his defiant snarl.

"Don't try and trick me, demon, I will not be fooled."

"One day..." the demon muttered, shaking the boy's head

with slow, pressured movements. "You think I'm the one who needs to be exorcised?"

"On the day of judgement–" Eddie persisted.

"On the day of judgement, it will be you that leads us!"

"On the day of judgement," Eddie repeated, even more forcefully. "We sinners will beg you to hear us as you hear us now."

He held out his cross and took his final stride toward his enemy.

"Give us peace and unity. Remove this demon and free this child."

The boy's face wrapped up into a visage of rage, defiant to the end.

"Leave this boy be, I ask you, my Lord. Remove this demon."

The boy's body stiffened to a rigid plank, its fingers curling. With a high screech, the child convulsed, stiffened more and more until, in a sudden snap, his body relaxed.

The room fell to tranquillity. A lucid calmness cast itself over them like a sunrise.

The boy breathed slowly, staring at the ceiling. Free at last.

Once the boy had been reunited with the mother and Eddie and Derek had received her gratitude, they made their way to Derek's car.

"What I don't understand," Eddie said, "were the things this demon was saying."

"Demons will say anything to defy you, Eddie. You need to learn not to listen to them."

"But if each demon keeps saying it?"

"Then they all know who you are and are saying the same thing to make you question it. Don't be fooled."

Eddie sighed, leaning against the car, Derek's answer clearly not good enough.

"Eddie, a demon is a devious thing, full of nothing but evil. Its sole purpose is to hurt us. You don't think they have some kind of organised defiance against someone as powerful as you?"

"I don't know. I guess."

"Eddie, you need to understand, there is no demon that can defeat you. There is nothing. And they will clutch at anything to change that."

Eddie nodded, soaking up the reassurance, starting to feel better.

"How is it you believe in me so much?" Eddie asked.

"Because I have seen what you can do. I have witnessed it."

"Yeah. It's just... I don't know."

Eddie turned to get into the car, full of doubt, until Derek put a hand on his arm to stop him.

"Well I do," he defiantly asserted. "You may have doubts in you, but I don't. My belief in you will never falter, Eddie. I promise."

MARCH 2003

THREE YEARS, THREE MONTHS SINCE
MILLENNIUM NIGHT

CHAPTER SIXTEEN

*O*nce again Martin stood unwillingly in the garden, numbing his mind into frantic concentration.

Glaring at the object before him. The garden bench was now wrecked pieces of wood, so he was forced to find an alternative, coming to him in the form of a dining chair. One that Derek had eagerly carried out from the kitchen.

First things first.

Concentrate on all the elements.

Sight.

The chair before him. Rustic, with a light-brown furnish. Clear green grass beneath it soaking up the rays of a bright sun.

Sound.

Birds singing. Nearby children playing. When really straining, there was even a faint hum of distant traffic.

Smell.

Flowers. Sweat.

Touch.

He flexed his hands, flowing them through a soft breeze, feeling the brush of gentle wind glide through his fingers.

Taste.

A faint taste of that morning's toothpaste.

Ready.

He concentrated on all of this, soaking it up, feeling the sun against his skin, listening to the birds, happy tweets of horny animals.

He moved his right arm in a circular motion.

The breeze.

His perspiration.

He moved it quicker.

The blades of grass sticking between his toes, the soft sink of soil beneath the sole of his foot.

He widened the radius of his arm's circular motion. A gold flickering circle had emerged, vague sparks bursting away like an electrical charge, the circle itself taking on a solid form, more and more solid with every circular motion, getting stronger with the increased speed of his arm.

The sun.

The blue sky.

The chair.

The wooden chair. Brown. Old. Uncomfortable. Sitting unknowingly across the garden, waiting for an attack.

The circle had taken its form. It had turned into a solid object he had conjured from pure awareness, from a complete absorption of his surroundings.

In a sudden thrust, he threw his open palm out, flinging the circle he had created toward the chair.

To Martin's astonishment, the chair did not explode. It remained sturdy. What's more, the circular magical binding flung itself around the chair.

Martin closed his fist and the circle tightened. It squeezed securely around the chair so that if the chair was alive there would be no way to escape, completely restricting the movement whilst leaving it intact.

Martin fell to his knees in inexplicable exhilaration.

It had worked.

The damn thing had worked.

It's actually doing it...

Martin closed his eyes and turned his face away, then opened his eyes again, expecting it to be a hallucination or a hopeful mirage.

It was still there.

Flicking like an uncaged wire of electricity, its voltage giving off sparks, it gripped firmly around the chair.

It's real...

So much working, so much trying, and he finally had it.

The flickers told him that the restraints weren't perfect yet, but that was fine, he could perfect it later. For now, he had actually done it.

He got up to go find Derek and tell him the great news.

Then a thought suddenly halted him. His smile faded, his body tensing again.

He remembered.

I'm going to have to use this spell on the heir.

Throwing a small circle around the chair was one thing. The heir was something else.

The flickers would have to go, as they would be a weakness the heir could easily penetrate. The size needed to be bigger, far grander — huge — to be able to fit around this creature. It would need to fly faster, otherwise, the heir would just beat it away.

Yes, it needed a lot of work.

Far more work.

But Martin had managed this. He had finally done it. A week ago he was getting incredibly frustrated, now he had the spell working.

But to get it to where he needed it to go…

It was an impossible task. It would take ten times as much as he'd put into it so far, at a minimum.

With a reluctant sigh, he stood. The positivity of his triumphant celebrations were over. Back to work.

He focussed on the object once more, taking in the elements.

CHAPTER SEVENTEEN

*A*nother dusty, flat slab of a book heaved open upon Derek's desk.

This plan was all good and well, but would it succeed?

An exorcism.

An exorcism that doesn't call to God, but to a soul.

How would it even work?

He filled his whisky tumbler and took a sip, not even feeling its sharp sting, such was his concentration. He placed his reading glasses on, grimacing at having to wear them; it had only been a few months ago that he'd had to acquire them, and the thought of growing old saddened him.

Then again, the luxury of growing old is one many of us may not be afforded...

Flicking through the pages of *The Rites of Exorcism,* he re-acclimatised himself with the process of removing a demon from a helpless body.

It had been a while.

He had given Eddie the knowledge then found himself no longer needed to perform these acts. Eddie had managed to banish a demon from a body in twice the speed and with less effort.

But it was time to return to it. To his roots. To how it all started.

He opened a chapter about the reasoning behind the process of an exorcism and found himself reading the words he had originally read when he began his endeavours to rid the world of hungry demons possessing their prey, almost two decades ago.

An exorcism's purpose is to tear two entities apart. Within possession, the soul of a victim has a demon latched onto it. You must separate the demon from the soul.

The body cannot exist without the soul, and the victim will be buried deep within. The exorcism consists of calling on God's strength to identify this soul and help pull it away from the demon.

DEREK LEANT BACK.

Thought deeply.

Pondered the various reasonings and thoughts behind these words.

By this theory, Eddie's soul would still be there.

It said that the body cannot exist without the soul. Therefore, the heir of Hell's body could not exist without Eddie' soul.

So it must be in there somewhere.

Buried very deep, maybe — but there.

It said that a possession means the soul has a demon latched onto it.

The issue was that Eddie's soul hadn't been latched onto by

a separate entity. They were both the same thing. The heir of Hell was not possessing Edward King – it *was* Edward King.

Normally an exorcism takes a demonic entity that has attached itself to a separate host. Could it still work, considering the heir and Eddie were not separate, but one and the same?

Could the process be performed in such a way that it separated the soul from the rest of the body, even if the soul belonged to that body?

Then again, an exorcism's purpose is to remove the evil from the good.

A soul is inherently good. Hell cannot create a soul, only Heaven can.

Therefore, it must be in there.

And by that logic, it could be separated.

Could be.

Derek mulled this over. He'd have to tear apart two things that are fastened together as one and the same. Unless the devil had to remove the soul when raising the heir. Unless the soul had already been ripped away and was being kept somewhere separate.

If it had already been ripped away, it would be looser, and easier to snatch off... but it would mean penetrating whatever protection the devil had put around it.

It was complicated, no doubt about it.

The one thing it confirmed was that Jenny was right.

There was still a piece of Eddie in there.

His soul.

That was the part they needed to appeal to.

That was the part Derek needed to reach.

It may not work.

Then again, it might.

He downed the rest of his whisky.

Slammed the glass down upon his coaster, the surface of which was peeling away.

The task was a daunting one to say the least.

To restrain the most powerful demon to ever have existed. Then to exorcise that demon. Then to plunge past the devil's defences. The devil's barriers.

Bloody hell, Derek. This is madness...

He had no choice.

He turned to the chapter on the prayers and became reacquainted with the ancient skill of the rites of exorcism.

He would need to know them thoroughly if he was to commit to this.

CHAPTER EIGHTEEN

*H*eaven was such a wonderful place, but it could be lonely if you kept looking to Earth. Seeing what so many people don't have.

Particularly for Cassy, who watched Martin trying again and again to produce the spell they needed to capture and fight the heir.

To exorcise it.

Being honest, Cassy wasn't entirely sure it was the best idea. It was radical, no denying that; but was it doable?

Then again, was killing the heir doable?

Cassy had felt Eddie's soul. She had felt it rip into her. He was there, she knew it.

But an exorcism to rid the heir of its own imprisoned soul…

The only other option was to kill the heir, and they had already realised that would fail.

Even with the powers Heaven had bestowed upon Martin, he was far less experienced than his opponent. And even if he had full control and ability over his inherent powers, he would only reach a stalemate with the heir; Heaven and Hell would always cancel each other out.

"You look solemn," came a familiar voice behind her.

"Why do you think that is?" she replied.

Gabrielle appeared at her side. Her long, black hair glided over her immaculate white dress, her luscious black skin smooth as silk.

"Come, join the others," Gabrielle said.

Cassy shook her head, holding back tears.

"This is no good," Gabrielle insisted. "There is nothing we can do for them now. They are on their own."

"Why?" Cassy demanded, lifting her head defiantly. She had never so much as challenged her, respecting the thousands of years Gabrielle had been doing God's work. Compared to her, Cassy's wings were so young. She just didn't understand.

"We offered Derek a way out. He turned it down."

"Yes, because he's doing our job. We should be fighting."

"You know God forbids it."

"But *why?*"

"Because it is not our job to meddle, you foolish child!" Despite being an angry retort, her voice was still soft and in control — something only a wise angel could achieve.

"I just don't get why we are supposed to stand back and watch as the devil unleashes Hell on Earth."

"Because that is the difference between us and Hell. The devil interferes directly with human dealings. We give them the tools, but to hold divine influence would be ungodly."

"Ungodly," Cassy scoffed.

She peered at an image of Martin, repeatedly trying his restraint spell, again and again. Each time growing increasingly annoyed because it was either not big enough, had too many sparks, or had a lack of power — whatever it was, she understood why he was getting frustrated.

A delinquent child plucked out of immaturity and plunged

into a war he didn't understand. What he had done, including all his hard work, whether he succeeded or failed, was remarkable.

And where were the servants of Heaven reassuring him of that?

"We need something for Martin," Cassy said. "Some kind of divine intervention. Even if he masters this thing, he's going to come up against a brick wall with the heir. The heir has had years of sitting back and driving Eddie's thoughts. Martin is a child plunged into this. He will lose."

Gabrielle remained silent. She looked to Earth also, watching Martin, feeling her pain.

"We have conceived him from Heaven. What more can we do?"

"I don't know, some kind of weapon, maybe?"

"Cassy, this is not up for discussion. We are here to do His bidding; that is it. Now please, come."

Cassy shook her head. "I'm not coming."

Gabrielle's face faltered with a flicker of distress.

"There is going to be a rapture, Cassy. The Earth is doomed. We have evacuated the most faithful, now it is time for us to move out of the way."

"Move out of the way? The devil rises and we are just going to move out of the way for him?"

"Cassy, are you coming?"

Cassy looked back into Gabrielle's eyes, those piercing, strikingly beautiful hazel eyes. So much wisdom, so much experience.

Who was she to challenge that?

But when you know in your heart what you must do…

"I am not," Cassy decided.

"You are not coming?"

She looked to Martin, then back to Gabrielle.

"No," Cassy confirmed. "I am going to stand with Derek.

With Martin. I am going to do what I can. Without interfering as you are so adamantly against."

"Cassy, once we have shut the door to Heaven from Earth, it will remain shut until it ends, if it ever does. Those gates will not reopen; you will not be allowed back in."

"Then I best hope it ends."

With a hesitation, Gabrielle nodded. There was no way to change Cassy's mind.

She stepped forward, putting her arms around Cassy, holding her in a tight embrace.

"Take care," Gabrielle said.

"I will."

Keeping her arms around Cassy, Gabrielle leant back and looked intently into her eyes.

"If you are going to put your faith in Eddie, as I see Derek is planning to do, you must keep that faith. The only chance you have is if Eddie plays his part too."

Cassy nodded. She felt herself crying. Gabrielle had been more than a friend. She had been a guide. It broke her heart to leave her; but it broke more that she was going knowing Gabrielle was not joining her. Her eyes welled up and she held Gabrielle tightly, wrapping her arms around her and bringing her in closely.

"You are a sweet child," Gabrielle spoke.

Before Cassy could respond, Gabrielle turned and walked a few steps until she faded away.

And with that, the stairs to the gates of Heaven faded.

Cassy couldn't fight. She couldn't interfere.

She was stuck in the world of mortals with a helpless fragility.

She did not know whether it was the right decision.

But she knew it was where she belonged.

APRIL 2003

CHAPTER NINETEEN

*E*verything came down to this.

Or, at least, that's what it felt like.

As Martin watched Derek sit at his desk, studying his book, he couldn't help but feel like it was the end.

They had been waiting for the heir to strike with a sense of foreboding helplessness. That at any time he could just rise up, bringing the demons of Hell with him, and unleash their tirade on Earth.

What could they do to stop the heir now?

The heir had wiped out their army. The most powerful supernatural influences in the world were dead. Yes, powerful people still remained on Earth, but they would all be second choices; all with far less ability than the ones that were already so easily slaughtered.

Now it was up to the powers Heaven had bestowed on Martin and the knowledge Derek had.

So there Derek was, studying the rites of exorcism. Even though Derek had performed hundreds of exorcisms, and witnessed almost as many whilst training Eddie, there he still was. Strengthening his knowledge. Being thorough.

That's why Derek was Martin's inspiration.

He was relentless. An ethic of constant hard work, something Martin had never had growing up; but something he had attempted to emulate.

Teachers at school nagged him. Punished him for doing nothing. They never gave education a purpose or a relevance, never gave him the patience to discover it's okay to make mistakes so long as they are learnt from.

But Father Douglas had. Douglas had stripped his dignity down to its bare bones and helped build the muscle around them.

And Derek.

Derek had never expected more than Martin could give.

And it was the same now.

If they died giving the world over to Hell and all its creations, but went down with the biggest fight they could muster, he knew Derek would still be proud.

Martin grew restless and began wandering the study. Looking over the dusty, broken leather of Derek's old books, the journals kept in a cupboard, and the drawers full of junk.

He realised he had never seen inside those drawers. Out of curiosity, he opened one.

He froze.

"Derek?" Martin said, alert.

"Yes?" Derek asked, not turning away from his book.

"What is this?" Martin asked, pointing to a revolver in Derek's drawer.

"What?" Derek glanced over his shoulder, noticed the gun, grinned, then returned his gaze back to his book. "It's a six-shooter revolver."

"Why do you have it?"

"Don't worry, it's just for show. The chambers are empty."

"Oh," Martin answered, feeling comforted. Then it struck him that it was still a gun, loaded or not.

He closed the drawer, deciding that there were many layers to Derek that he would never truly be able to unfold.

A warm hand rested itself on Martin's shoulder. He recognised the soft touch, and turned to see the beautiful face of Cassy.

"Cassy?" he prompted, surprised to see her.

Derek turned, equally perplexed.

"Cassy?"

"Hello, Derek," she said knowingly, smiling back at him.

"What are you doing here?"

"Is that how you greet me?"

Derek chuckled heartily, but it quickly faded.

"The evacuation is complete. I thought that included all of the angels."

"It did. I told them I wouldn't go."

"You what?"

Derek rose, stepping forward, staring at her intently.

"My place is not hiding away in Heaven with a God who does nothing to help. My place is fighting with you." She turned with a graceful smile toward Martin. "With both of you."

Martin grinned. He was astonished.

"If you'll have me, that is."

"Of course," Martin answered, beaming at Derek.

"So where are we with this?"

"Oh, yes." Derek quickly readjusted and picked up his bulky book. "I've been studying the rites of exorcism again, looking to see if there was anything else we could do, any stronger prayer I could serve."

"And?"

Derek shrugged.

"I have a question," Martin announced. "If the angels are hidden away with God, will the exorcism work?"

"What do you mean?"

"Isn't an exorcism calling on God to remove a demon from its victim's body?"

Derek nodded.

"Well, in that case, ain't God going to be hidden away? I mean, how would he answer?"

Cassy looked to Derek, realising that she hadn't thought of this either.

"Maybe," Derek confirmed.

"But how?" Cassy interjected.

"Because we are not going to be calling on God to free Eddie from the demon's body. It would do no good, for the reasons you have stated, but also because we are not removing a demon from its victim. Instead, we are removing the victim's soul from its demonic body. We will need to reach out to that soul with our prayers, rather than to God."

"I don't understand."

"We will not be praying to God to exorcise the demon. We are going to be calling on Eddie himself."

CHAPTER TWENTY

*T*he room filled with silence. A few moments of contemplation reflecting upon Derek's statement.

Cassy looked from Martin, to Derek, then back again, perplexed.

They were going to call on Eddie?

It was either genius or reckless — Cassy was still undecided. It hadn't been attempted, calling on anyone but God to remove something — but in theory, it should work. If Eddie's soul was trapped away somewhere, they would need to call on it, grant it access to return.

Then it struck Cassy — the overpowering flaw of this idea.

"So, your hypothesis is that you could exorcise the soul from the demon's body, detach it and create a new entity," Cassy thought aloud to Derek. "So you would then have two conscious beings — the heir of Hell, and Eddie's soul. Correct?"

"Spot on," Derek confirmed, nodding enthusiastically.

"The only issue," Cassy continued, "is Eddie's soul. We don't know what form it would take."

"What do you mean?"

"The human soul is not a human. The soul's conscious mind

has the ability to project its own body with its own mind, so it can see itself as human — but it is not."

"Not what?" Martin interjected.

"Human. The soul, in its truest form, is merely a ball, made up of elements and supernatural components. You could very well remove the soul from the heir so that Eddie, as the soul, can defeat the heir. Only issue is…"

"… He wouldn't be able to defeat him in the form of a soul," Derek finished, bowing his head and closing his eyes in disappointment. "He would just be a ball of energy."

"I really do not understand what you guys are on about," Martin announced.

Derek and Cassy exchanged a glance, sub-consciously deciding who would explain to Martin in laymen's terms what the issue was.

"If we managed to exorcise Eddie's soul," Derek told him, "the soul would not return in a recognisable form, and wouldn't be able to defeat the heir."

"Oh," Martin said, leaning against the desk, his face turning to that of disappointment.

Cassy's initial excitement faded with the prospect of what they could have done. What other option did they have? How else could they defeat the antichrist, but with a piece of himself?

"Is there really nothing we can do about it?" Cassy asked.

Derek's pointing finger jolted upright, a complex thought striking him.

"What?" Cassy asked.

"There is a way," Derek announced.

"Okay?" Cassy replied, made anxious by Derek's tentative look.

"But you're not going to like it."

Cassy knew instantly where this was going.

"No, Derek, no," she insisted, standing and waving her

arms. "I am an angel. We fight in Heaven's name. There is no way."

"What?" Martin asked.

Derek turned to Martin and explained to him, knowing he couldn't look at Cassy while he suggested what he was about to suggest.

"There is a way to turn a soul into human form that I read about a while ago. Only, it's… it's not…"

"Not what, Derek?"

"Not something God would approve of. To turn a soul, something made out of Heaven, into a mortal form, goes against the rules of Heaven. It could only be done with devil worship."

"Why doesn't Heaven approve?"

"Because that soul already had its turn in mortal form. It's not allowed to be returned; it is supposed to pass on."

"I can't believe you're even suggesting this," Cassy interrupted, feeling her temperature rise and her blood boil. "This is sacrilege! God would not approve."

"With all due respect, where is your God now?"

Cassy was silenced. As true as his point was, Cassy was not prepared to stand there and entertain the option of using evil in any way.

They would lose far more than just the world if they allowed Satanism into their battle.

"I'm not suggesting that we do it–"

"I don't give a damn what you are suggesting."

"Cassy," Martin tried. "I… I don't know." He turned to Derek. "How would we even be able to use Hell to do this? I mean, you may not have noticed, but we aren't really on their side, are we?"

"I don't know, Martin, to be honest," Derek answered. "I was just thinking aloud."

"Well stop it, now!" Cassy demanded. "Stop it, right now!

Turning a soul to human form is the devil's work; it is unnatural to how a soul is created. We find the heavenly way to do this. There must be a way — there *must* be."

"And if there isn't?"

The question hung in the air like poisonous gas.

Cassy's fists clenched, her head frantically shaking in defiance.

"Why don't we sleep on this?" Derek suggested. "We are all tired. It's late. We need to clear our minds and think through this with clear thoughts."

"There is nothing to think of."

"Then what do you suggest, Cassy?"

Cassy bowed her head. Closed her eyes.

"I will go to Gabrielle tonight," she decided. "Hope she hasn't entered Heaven's gate yet. See what she says."

"Hah!" Derek laughed forcibly. "And how much help has she been, huh?"

"I will talk to her. Ask if there is anything else that can be done, any other way."

"Yeah, you do that," Derek answered with seething eyes, more hostile than he had intended.

She went to speak, but chose against it. She turned and left, making her way out of the house and into the street, in disbelief of what they could potentially become.

CHAPTER TWENTY-ONE

*D*erek's house was at peace. A full moon cast a serene glow over the house of tranquillity. The house was still and calm.

Except, it wasn't.

The silence of the hallway was filled with absent chaos.

Martin rocked back and forth in his bed, unable to sleep, troubled by thoughts sweeping around his mind like a hive of angry bees.

Derek was finally dozing. His mind was cluttered, but he was exhausted, and much in need of the sleep. His long absence from rest had finally forced a light slumber.

Neither of them noticed the lock on the front door being picked, or the door being creaked open into a soundless hallway.

Bandile treaded into the house softly and carefully, wary not to apply pressure to a creaky floorboard or to knock any ornament or artefact balanced carefully on an unsteady piece of furniture.

Dexter and Bagsy swiftly followed. Dexter's face was full of concentration, obediently following their leader, looking back and forth, observing every shadow and every movement.

Bagsy was less subtle. His grin widened with every step he took, taking sadistic pleasure at the thought of what they were going to do once they found their victims. He secretly hoped that they weren't cooperative — that way he could torture them more. Maim them. Tear off pieces flesh and watch as he forced them to eat it.

Nothing gave him a bigger thrill than a humiliated and helpless victim. It gave him a buzz of adrenaline that no high could otherwise outdo.

Bandile withdrew an Okapi knife. With its brown handle and large, pointed blade, this was a South African knife he had bought fifteen years ago, initially for hunting. He'd even had his wife's first name engraved on the blade, though that name had since faded, along with his memory of her. Still, he held it tightly in his grip, treasuring his weapon along with the sentimentality he attached to it.

He placed a soft foot on the bottom step, feeling it creak and withdrawing his foot promptly. Signalling at the other two with his eyes to indicate that they should skip that step, he placed a soft foot on the step above. Slowly, but surely, they made their way up the stairs and onto the landing.

The moon cast a generous light through an opening in the curtains, casting a humble glow down the corridor. There were two closed bedroom doors that Bandile assumed were home to Derek and Martin.

As much as he would have liked to end his history with Derek with a flourish, it was Martin he was after. The only one who could oppose the heir.

This was Bandile's ticket. His safe ticket through to a high place in Hell. His salvation, his promise to the devil that he was worthy of being spared an eternity of torture and torment in their fiery pits. The only way he could ensure that the devil would look kindly upon him. That he would be saved when Hell opened and demons swarmed the earth.

He had to prove himself.

Even after all he had done. The Devil's Three was part of a deal — he needed to do something extra, something that provided true evidence of his loyalty.

Bandile placed a gentle palm against the door handle, delicately pushing it open.

There on the bed, his eyes peacefully closed, lay Derek. He looked to have aged significantly in the short time since the ritual, evidence of grey in his hair and further wrinkles on his face.

He nodded to the other two. They stepped forward to detain Derek, as Bandile turned back into the corridor.

Bandile strode to the other closed door at the end of the corridor, to forcibly gain entry to the room that must contain Martin.

Sweaty in anticipation.

Licking his lips as the door grew near.

He clutched his knife. Flexed his fingers.

One swipe into the neck of Martin is all it would take.

No hesitation.

No point taking him hostage.

Then the devil would see that he was worthy.

He kicked opened the door and stormed into the room, pulling the duvet back, lifting his knife into the air, and–

The bed was empty.

The boy wasn't there.

Bandile searched the room, turning the bed upside down, opening the wardrobe, throwing the desk over in a fit of anger.

He burst out the room and into the next, searching everywhere, opening every door, analysing every corner.

The bathroom was empty.

Every damn room in the house was empty.

Bandile marched back into Derek's room, where the man crouched at the feet of Dexter and Bagsy with a bloody nose.

Bandile tucked his large hand securely around Derek's neck, lifting him up and pinning him against the wall. His arm shook with anger, his face curled up into an aggressive sneer, sickened to the gut with fury that the boy he was after was nowhere to be found.

"Where is he?" Bandile demanded, growling into the face of Derek.

"Where — is — who?" Derek stuttered, struggling for breath under the force of Bandile's heavy palm.

"The boy! *Where is he?!*"

"I — have — no — idea…"

Bandile threw Derek to the ground.

"Do what you need to," he instructed Bagsy, knowing he would enjoy this task most. "Remove every tooth, every nail, and every limb if you have to. Find out where he is!"

Bagsy's smirk danced upon his face with a fluttering excitement.

"Oh, boss," he sang in a disjointed tune. "You are too kind…"

CHAPTER TWENTY-TWO

*T*urns out having to concentrate on every sight, sound, smell, taste and touch, day in and day out, meant that Martin could tell when something was amiss. A distant shuffle, a barely audible movement, resounding delicately from down the hallway, became a piercing clang in his ears.

He crept from his bed and to the door, opening it with a small crack.

Three men. A large black man, a man with a beard, and a man covered in intimidating tattoos. Edging through the hallway, toward Derek's door.

Martin grew alarmed. His whole body stiffened into fight or flight, his mind rapidly firing through his possible next steps.

Fight them?

Hurt them?

Kill them?

They were not demons. They were humans.

Martin's powers were not for killing humans.

It was a line Martin had never thought about crossing.

They opened Derek's door. Led by the large black man carrying a large knife.

Shit.

He looked around himself for a weapon.

Nothing.

He could always get Derek's revolver.

But it was empty.

No.

I am the weapon.

He could conjure fire. He could throw wind. He could manipulate his surroundings into chaos.

But Derek...

There was no way he could guarantee Derek's safety if he was to burst out and start a fight.

He was going to need to be more strategic.

He ran to the window, opening it and looking below. It was a steep drop. Though he was pretty sure he could dangle down, out of sight.

But what then?

How would he get back into the house?

Hearing footsteps heading toward his room, he knew he was running out of time. He needed to make a decision; however instinctive it may end up being.

He climbed out of the window and dangled on the ledge, clinging on with the tips of his fingers. He leant his feet against the wall and reached up a spare arm, closing the window behind, being careful to leave a slight gap he could still use.

He looked down.

If he fell from this, he could land on his neck.

Suddenly the vision of numerous nightmare scenarios ran through his mind.

He closed his eyes. Held on tight. Calmed his mind.

Heavy stomping pounded the floor of his room. Doors slammed open and shut. Banging of furniture being upturned and items being thrown bashed against the walls, shaking the ledge Martin loosely hung onto.

He felt his fingers slip.

Hearing the heavy footsteps grow fainter, he lifted himself back up, peering into the room.

It was empty.

He opened the window and crept back inside.

CHAPTER TWENTY-THREE

*D*erek blinked the blood out of his eye. He tilted his head, trying to avoid the trail of blood trickling from the top of his head landing in his eye again.

He spat a mouthful of blood to the floor, feeling a tooth dislodge with it. An absent softness announced itself at the back of his lower jaw where the tooth had previously been.

The skinny man with the sadistic grin and devilish inking stomped on his head once more and he saw black.

He came back around again in what he was sure was only a few seconds later. He lay on his back, staring up at a wall that spun in circle after circle.

"Thank you, Bagsy," came a voice Derek recognised. A thick South African accent.

It could only be one man.

A sudden jolt shocked his body into alertness.

"No, it can't be…"

Bandile Thato knelt beside Derek's head. Derek turned to look at his old friend and enemy, feeling the muscles in his neck tighten and his jaw stiffen as he did, his body aching from the pain of numerous beatings.

Visions of Bandile imparting wisdom on him filled the front of his mind; wise words guiding him on what he should do with his concerns about Eddie — all the while manipulating him.

"Hello, Derek," came the thick accent of the man he had once called a confidant.

"You bastard…" Derek muttered, gurgling on a mouthful of blood.

"Where is Martin?" Bandile asked, his voice remaining blank and void of feeling.

"I trusted you…"

"Where — is — Martin?"

"Go to Hell…" Derek spluttered, dropping his head away.

Bandile nodded to the one he had called Bagsy.

The scrawny man mounted Derek, holding something high in his hand. Derek tried to make out what it was. It was silver, rusted. Two pieces of metal pressed together, creating a high-pitched ping as they retracted and collapsed. Such a sound had never felt more terrifying.

As Derek's vision readjusted, he made it out. It was a clamp of some kind.

Bagsy held the clamp over Derek's two front teeth, pressing it firmly around them, ready to do his worst.

Derek closed his eyes.

He had to endure.

He had to give Martin a chance.

"I will ask you one more time," Bandile said. "Where is the boy?"

Derek scrunched his face up, wincing from the expectation of pain to come. Getting ready. Preparing himself for whatever sacrifice he had to make.

But Bagsy was interrupted.

The door flung open. Martin burst through.

Derek's heart sank.

No...

He had prayed Martin had made his escape. There was too much riding on his existence.

And a smile raising slowly upon Bandile's face told Derek just what was at risk.

Taking the opportunity of distraction, Derek lifted his arm and sank his fist into Bagsy's face, knocking the bony mess onto his side. Derek rolled onto his front, moaning from the pain in his arm — he wasn't sure he'd ever actually thrown a punch before. He managed to push himself to his knees.

Bandile held a knife by his side.

Martin glared at it. Derek could see him concentrating, could see him getting his gift ready.

Derek couldn't let him do it.

To murder goes against Heaven. Derek wasn't even sure that if Martin committed such a cardinal sin, his powers would even remain.

Martin raised his hands, nursing a ball of fire in each one, glaring intently at the intruders, readying his fiery weapons.

"No, Martin!" Derek cried out.

Martin looked to Derek, confused.

"You cannot kill them," Derek pleaded. "They are humans, not demons."

Martin appeared thrown by this, dropping his hands to his side.

The bearded man dove upon Martin, taking him to the floor, punching him in the back of the head until his eyes closed and his face faded into submission.

Bandile took this opportunity to raise his knife, ready to plunge it into his victim's neck.

CHAPTER TWENTY-FOUR

*C*assy marched through paradise, venomous rage in her eyes.

A beautiful landscape encompassed the entry to Heaven, fruitful trees waving in a silent breeze, the scent of wildflowers complementing the pure air.

Cassy ignored it, staring contemptuously at Gabrielle who appeared from inside the gates, come to see what the commotion was about.

"Cassy, have you changed your mind?" Gabrielle asked. "I fear it may be too late."

"I haven't changed my mind, Gabrielle," Cassy insisted as she stormed toward her. "I know the gates of Heaven are still; that is not why I am here."

"Then what are you after?"

"We have a plan to bring Eddie's soul back, but we need help."

Gabrielle grew puzzled.

"But – how are they going to manage that?"

"With an exorcism."

"I don't think you understand, Cassy – how are they going

to carry out an exorcism when they are either dead or condemned?"

Cassy was stumped, taken aback by the nonsensical words of her supposed friend.

"What are you talking about?" Cassy retorted. "They are not dead! And to be condemned they would have to commit an act that went against Heaven, and whilst we have spoken about this, we have not–"

"Cassy," Gabrielle interrupted. "I don't think you know, do you?"

"Know what?"

Gabrielle waved her arm in a swift, graceful movement, revealing a glimpse of earth.

Cassy saw them.

With a sudden bolt of terror, an entwining twist of her absent guts, she fell to her knees, watching as Derek and Martin were tortured. Hurt. Beaten into bloody messes.

Cassy waved the vision away, unable to take anymore. Her legs felt weak, shaking under the pressure of the burden of what she had seen.

She tried to get back to her feet but fell once more, Gabrielle reaching through the gate to support her.

"And you can just watch this?" she shouted at Gabrielle.

"Cassy, lower your voice; these are the gates of Heaven."

"I don't give a damn about the gates of Heaven!" Cassy roared, throwing Gabrielle's helpful hands off her.

"Don't you see, Cassy? They only have two ways out of the situation they are in. Either they die, or they have to kill their captors."

"And if they have to kill them, then they are going to Hell, right? Is that what you're saying?"

"Not just that, dear child — they would be condemned."

Cassy closed her eyes in frustration, willing herself to be calm as she realised what Gabrielle was saying.

"If they were to kill, they would no longer be worthy of Heaven. And any exorcism would prove redundant."

Gabrielle gave a sympathetic smile and a nod, which only infuriated Cassy further.

"You are all pathetic, you know that?" Cassy spat. "You called me to be an angel to make a difference in this war. But... You. God. The whole legion of angels — you don't do shit!"

"Cassy, I understand you are hurting, but I compel you to watch your tongue, or He may deem you as being blasphemous."

Cassy laughed. She couldn't help it. She choked on her mocking laughter, in utter disbelief. Her whole belief system, the angel she had become, what she had been made to represent — it all came crumbling down around her.

"Unbelievable. They are fighting in your name, fighting your war for you, and you would condemn them to Hell?"

"With a heavy heart."

"To Hell with your heavy heart, Gabrielle."

"This conversation is over," Gabrielle decided, turning her back on Cassy and walking back into her sanctuary.

"So that's it, huh?" Cassy cried out. "They are in a situation, you don't want to help, so that's Earth done. The whole world wiped out. Because Heaven can't be bothered to help them!"

Gabrielle paused, turning around gracefully and, even though she always retained her air of calmness, a slight air of frustration began to creep through.

"The human race has lasted longer than most."

Cassy shook her head and turned away, marching away from the gates of Heaven.

"Where are you going?" Gabrielle asked.

"To help them!" Cassy said, spinning back around before resuming her walk away.

"If you interfere, if you allow these actions, if you condone an act of murder — you will be forever condemned from Heaven, Cassy, I hope you realise that."

Cassy continued walking away, ignoring Gabrielle's pleading.

"When Heaven's gates reopen, you may have retained your wings, but you will no longer be allowed entry."

Cassy paused. Turning around slowly, she decided this would be her last attempt at reasoning with the unreasonable.

"I think I understand, you know," she said slowly and quietly, but with a toxic edge. "God can't involve himself in ungodly acts because He needs His pawns to do it. That way He can keep His hands clean, keep Himself holy. It's always people sacrificing their pledges to Him, He never kills that sacrifice himself."

"Cassy–"

"If He doesn't have the gumption, I will. And I will save Martin and Derek from either fate. And you will look on and say that you tried to help me. Then, by the same reasoning, I will look up and say that I also attempted to help you."

Cassy walked away.

Gabrielle said nothing.

She stood there, watching God's faithful servant disappear into the distance.

It didn't matter whether Gabrielle agreed with Cassy or not.

It mattered that Gabrielle carried out His actions.

His demands.

However difficult that was.

However much she may oppose it; she was an angel, she was His soldier.

She was to take orders.

Cassy rebelled, but she could not.

Still, she found it hard to return into the secluded harmony behind those gates.

Knowing the gates would be firmly shut soon, she struggled to find her legs striding inside.

Instead, she found herself poised on the outside, struggling with the movement, Cassy's words bouncing repeatedly around her thoughts.

CHAPTER TWENTY-FIVE

*B*andile's knife hung in the air for what seemed like an eternity. Martin watched it, poised for battle, but conflicted by the words Derek had urgently bestowed on him.

He had to ask himself — could he take a human life? Was he prepared to make that sacrifice?

So far he had killed demons, entities made of pure evil, which had not worn down his conscience whatsoever. But killing three people to save his and Derek's life…

Was he prepared to do it?

Yes.

Could he?

…

Derek's eyes widened in what felt like slow motion. Bandile's knife came thundering down with a steady uncertainty that made Martin's heart beat quickly.

Martin was pinned down by one of them. Seconds earlier and he would have conjured fire ready to set each of them alight, to burn them to ashes within seconds. Now, he was restrained, and unable to concentrate astutely enough to re-conjure the elements, unable to move his arms in such a way that they would answer.

The question that ripped across his mind was — could he live with himself knowing that he could have prevented Derek's death?

Fate had not been in their favour so far.

Then, before the question could be answered, a sudden bright light encapsulated the room. Martin instinctively flinched away, hiding his face, shielding himself from the salvo of light.

As the light died down he opened his eyes.

Cassy.

With her elegant demeanour and a bright-white backlight beaming from the edge of her skin, she stood over them with a look of determination, thwacking the man holding the knife in the air to the floor.

Martin felt himself free of restraints, the man pinning him down having instinctively loosened his grip to shield himself from the light long enough for Martin to burst to his feet.

He circled his hands, flickering embers of fire, readying his attack. He would not be caught again.

Cassy raised her hand.

"No!" she commanded.

"What?" Martin said, enraged that both she and Derek had instructed him not to defend himself. He was eager to fight, and not at all ready to give in.

"Don't," she commanded, a look of begging in her eyes. "You can't. Nothing will work if you take a human life."

"We have no choice!"

"No, Martin, *I* have no choice. I am saving you from yourself."

Before Martin could object any further, she had taken the knife off the bearded man and plunged it into his throat.

He collapsed on the floor, clutching onto his bleeding neck, blood pouring through the cracks of his hands. He wriggled and thrashed, bashing the furniture of the room with his feet, but knew it would do nothing as he reached his violent end.

Martin watched as the man's life fell through his fingers.

He watched, knowing he could not have done that.

Knowing that causing this pain was not something he could have brought himself to do to another human.

The scrawny tattooed man behind him went to attack but Cassy got to him first, sticking the knife into his gut, then across his throat.

Blood splattered over her translucent heavenly white gown, staining the image of the angelic.

In the instant the man died, her bright-white light faded.

The large black man readied his grand knife, facing Cassy, ready for a fight.

Cassy rose her knife into the air.

"No!" Derek demanded, standing, holding an arm out to Cassy.

"No Derek, it has to be me that does this."

"No, we cannot kill him!" Derek pleaded. "We need him."

"What for?"

"His name is Bandile Thato. He is a devil worshipper."

Cassy realised what Derek's plan was and dropped her knife to her side.

Bandile dove his knife toward her, but Martin leapt to his feet, rotating his hand, and within seconds he had conjured a restraint spell and thrown the gold circle around Bandile. It tightened around his chest and rose him into the air, his legs dangling pathetically. Bandile struggled against his incarceration, but the supernatural binding was too secure for a human to fight.

Martin pumped his fist in the air, celebrating that he had successfully implemented the restraint spell. Questions still arose as to whether it was strong enough to hold the antichrist, but there were no questions as to whether it would be strong enough to bind a human for as long as they wanted.

Bandile was theirs. Captive and helpless.

Derek stepped forward, looking Bandile up and down. Bandile's lip curled upwards in an aggressive snarl, his head shaking slowly.

"Hello, old friend," Derek spoke.

Bandile's snarl grew, a rebellious insolence wiping across his livid features.

"You're going to do us a favour."

CHAPTER TWENTY-SIX

*B*andile's eyes fluttered like the wings of a moth, adjusting to the dimness of the light. A distant dripping plagued his ears with an incessancy he could do nothing about. His clothes stank like damp, as did the room, and the footsteps of his captors echoed throughout.

His vision finally came into focus. He looked around, peering at his surroundings, trying to make an assumption as to where he was.

It was Derek's basement. He was sure of it.

He went to move. He couldn't. He looked down.

Rope wrapped around his chest multiple times.

Derek and the boy stood before him. Both with their arms folded, feet shoulder-width apart, their faces displaying resolute glares.

Bandile couldn't help but snigger.

Derek was a well-spoken professor, and this other one was a pathetic little kid. And there they were, trying to look tough, like some ridiculous mock-up action men. The imbeciles were anything but intimidating, and he couldn't help but enjoy the hilarity, despite his evident incarceration.

"You two are fucking pitiful," he chuckled.

He turned to his right and saw a woman stood before him. He knew from the white dress and the radiant skin that she was an angel, except... the dress was blood-splattered. Her illumination had faded. She was...

She was being denied Heaven.

Because she had killed his cult members. His poor excuse for assailants.

He threw his head back and guffawed.

"You lost your entry to the Promise Land!" he cackled mockingly. "Because you killed Dexter and Bagsy!"

He threw his head to the side, belting out his guffaws.

"They were pathetic!" he cackled. "You could have gotten a fucking rat to kill them! And you sacrificed everything..."

He continued to laugh, wailing uproariously. He could feel rope tight against his chest, his ankles restrained to the bottom of his chair, and handcuffs clamped securely around his wrists. He wasn't getting out of this situation, so the only thing he could do was incense them with his interminable hysterics.

"Laugh all you want," Derek said. "We have you restrained. You're not going anywhere."

"And what are you going to do to me? Huh?" Bandile taunted them. "Kill me?"

Derek glanced at Cassy and they exchanged a look. Bandile could tell that they had a plan. He could also tell from how Martin was left out of the look that he was seen as the inexperienced one of the trio.

In fact, it wouldn't have surprised Bandile if Martin had been left out of the loop entirely.

"You guys are idiots," Bandile said. "You fall for everything. And what, you think this little squirt stands a chance against the heir of Hell?"

"I'm not going to kill the heir of Hell," Martin said.

"Oh, yeah?"

"No," Derek took over. "Edward King is."

Bandile fell silent.

Had he heard them correctly?

Edward King was going to kill the heir of Hell?

But…

Edward King is the heir of Hell.

"What are you on about?" he demanded.

"You are going to do something for us," Derek continued. "Something to help kill the heir of Hell."

"Why would I do that?"

"We are going to exorcise the soul of Edward King out of the heir of Hell so it can kill the antichrist," Derek continued, ignoring Bandile's irrelevant question. "Only there is an issue."

Bandile grinned. He knew where this was going.

"A soul can't take human form, can it?" he pointed out. "And it is an ungodly act. Heaven won't turn something as beautiful as a soul into something as weak and mortal as a human body. It goes against Heaven to return life to a body where there was none. So many reasons they won't do it… so you need a devil worshipper to do it."

"That's right."

"And that is where I come in, my old friend." Bandile smiled widely, watching Derek grimace from his reference to him as an old friend.

"Yes. And you are going to do this."

"Tell me why I would do this, Derek. Please."

Derek sighed and took a few steps toward Bandile, focussing his stare on the man he once trusted.

"If you repent," Derek explained. "Ask forgiveness, then prove this by bringing back the man who can defeat the antichrist, that would be your path to Heaven. And it would be your *only* path to Heaven."

"Why would I–" Bandile began to object, then stopped.

A thought hit him.

He couldn't care less about a path to Heaven. He wanted a throne in Hell. It was the only way, the only path after the horrific actions he had taken.

But maybe this was that path.

If he led them to believe that he was going to do this for them... then didn't... meaning they would be full of hope, then left helpless for the antichrist to kill them...

They may just be stupid enough to believe that he wouldn't be deceptive. That he would want this path to Heaven.

Derek Lansdale had already proven that he was a gullible man.

"Okay," Bandile said. "I will do this."

Derek nodded.

"Good." Derek glanced at the other two. "Until that time comes."

He nodded and turned, ascending the stairs. Martin and Cassy followed, turning the light off.

Bandile was left in darkness, feeling something soft scurry past his ankles.

CHAPTER TWENTY-SEVEN

 $\mathcal{M}$ oisture hung in the air in that way it always does in church; loose damp that clings to your clothes. The vast, open room loomed overhead with its great architecture, reverberating all footsteps and rebounding voices against its stone walls.

But there were no voices.

And Cassy didn't create heavy footsteps. An attribute of being an angel was that her feet were gentle.

She made her way to the front of the church and paused.

The tall crucifix stood over her. A symbol of comfort giving her nothing but rage.

So, this is where people came to pray. To ask for forgiveness from a God who doesn't listen and for help from angels that never come.

For Cassy, it wasn't an issue of whether humans should believe in their God. It was a question of whether humans would want to.

Why worship a God that doesn't listen?

A God who chooses to hide those he deems good enough to survive, and lets those he deems unworthy perish.

A God who has buildings devoted to him, but doesn't listen to the people who built them.

A God who gave them the world with painful death. Illnesses. A world where animals have to kill animals to survive.

She was one of his disciples, but even so, she was disillusioned with the concept of faith.

Now she had been banished from Heaven. She was an angel without a home, without a purpose. She had an angel's life in a human's body and it was all for nothing.

Thanks to the God they fought in the name of.

But she wasn't here for God.

She wasn't here to ask for his help.

She dropped to her knees and bowed her head, closing her eyes. A moment of solitude, thinking about he who matters most.

"Eddie," she whispered, so faintly only she could hear it. "Please, listen to me."

She tightened her closed eyes. Tears punched the backs of her eyelids, endeavouring to get out, but she refused. She was here to help, not cry.

"Eddie, we need you. Please just hear me."

She lifted her head, opening her eyes. Tears blurred her vision.

"Eddie, you must–"

"You don't call, you don't write…" came a familiar voice singing out bouncily behind her. "The only time you want to talk to me is in a lousy bleedin' church."

Cassy gasped.

Her hands stiffened. Her arms grew rigid, her breath stuck in her throat.

It couldn't be…

"What's the matter, sis'? Aren't you gonna say hi?"

Cassy stood, sweaty-palmed, shaking legs. She slowly turned, dreading the sight she was about to see.

There he sat.

On a bench, three rows back. A sharp black suit and a cocky smile that didn't suit Eddie at all. He looked like her brother. He had the same pitch of voice. The same hair, the same face. But his mannerisms were different. The tone of his voice was sadistically playful. The glint in his eye was neither happy nor charming, but arrogant and conceited.

He had the face of her brother, but she knew that was only to torment her further.

"I'm an angel, you can't hurt me," she said, assuring herself more than him. Despite the sentiment of what she said, her lip still quivered and her voice still shook.

"Oh, yeah?"

"Yes. You can't."

"I can't *physically* hurt you, is that what you're saying?"

"Exactly."

"But that doesn't mean I can't hurt you."

Cassy shook her head. He couldn't hurt her, she knew it. There was an agreement.

Then the sad realisation hit her.

There are no truces in war.

"How about your wise and knowing friend, Derek?" he proposed, sticking out his bottom lip, sitting back and draping his arm leisurely over the side of the bench. "Would be a real shame if I hurt him to hurt you, wouldn't it?"

Her eyes narrowed. She shook her head in terror, glaring at him with fearful malice.

"And your little boy, Martin," he continued, nodding with confirmation. "The little boy made by Heaven, the one who's meant to take me on. A pathetic attempt by your pathetic God to make it seem like he gives a shit."

Cassy looked past him, to the far door. Could she get there in time?

"You know why it is I can't hurt you?" he asked, standing up and sauntering cockily toward her. "Because many thousands of years ago, Heaven and Hell made an agreement that demons and angels would not fight, so as to avoid a complete mass genocide in which no one would win or lose."

Cassy backed up as he crept closer, bumping into the giant cross with the dead Jesus attached.

"But what if I didn't right feel like obeying the rules? You know, seeing as we're about to break pretty much every treaty we've ever had."

His hands flung to her throat, squeezing tightly. Her arms shook frantically, a sense of doom seizing up and down her spine and in through the pit of her stomach. She could feel that she was truly in the presence of evil.

"Even though you don't breathe," he whispered callously, his face within an inch of hers. "It still hurts that I strangle you. Even though you don't have a heart that beats, it would still cause you incredible pain if I were to rip that heart out and squash it beneath my foot."

She closed her eyes, scrunching up her face as if preparing for impact.

Is this what I'm going to contribute? Is this what I came back for?

To be a coward in the face of that which she was helping to oppose?

"Eddie..." she whimpered. "Eddie, please, I need your help..."

It was a long shot, and it stank of desperation — but if Eddie was there, if he was able to control something — he could show her right now.

"Eddie's not here right now," the false face of her brother retorted, grinning wildly.

He lifted her into the air and threw her down the aisle,

watching her slide across her back until she hit a pew and collapsed into a heap.

"I've decided to end this," he announced, strutting toward her. "I've decided I'm just going to kill everyone. Got bored, I guess."

She clambered to her knees, dragging her shaking body to its feet.

"But first, I need to know where to find your little friend."

Cassy shook her head, scrambling to her feet and running away. Within a flash Eddie had shot across the church and halted before her, causing her to collapse against his fake chest. He put his arms around her, squeezing tightly, wrapping her in a merciless embrace.

"I miss this. When we just used to cuddle."

"That wasn't you, it was Eddie."

"Oh, I was always there. Hiding. Waiting for my time to shine."

"I will *never* give up my friends. You'll have to break the truce and kill me."

"Not being funny, but I was planning on doing that anyway."

She shook her head.

Please, Eddie. If you are there, just, please...

"How about we take a trip?"

Feeling her chest tighten under the pressure of being squeezed, she winced, and she started to feel the first bit of human pain since she had ascended to Heaven. Large spikes grew out of his body, digging into her, wrapping around her, ensuring she was painfully secured.

In a shot, he soared them into the air and fired them through the church roof faster than she could handle.

APRIL 2002

TWO YEARS, FOUR MONTHS SINCE MILLENNIUM
NIGHT

CHAPTER TWENTY-EIGHT

*T*he door swung so hard into the adjacent wall that the handle left a dent in the poor paint job. Kelly burst through, punching the door away as it rebounded back against her, sending it swinging on its hinges.

She folded her arms, shaking her head, storming into the kitchen. She bit her lip, ferociously searching the room for something to quell her rumination.

Eddie followed, edging slowly into the room with an air of calmness that only incensed her further. He steadied the flapping door and looked at her hopefully.

"Kelly–" he attempted.

"No!" she interrupted, gesticulating her arms wildly. "No, you do not get to walk in here all calm and try and be the voice of reason!"

"Excuse me?"

"Don't excuse me me, you know exactly what I am on about!"

Eddie raised an eyebrow. She sneered at him, refolding her arms and turning away irritably.

He sank his hands into his pockets, and took a moment,

gathering his thoughts. He avoided eye contact with her for a few seconds, staring at the corner of the room as he tried to figure out what could possibly be the right thing to say at this moment.

"Look, I'm just trying to help."

"Well, you can't! You don't know what it's like to be possessed!"

"Don't know what it's like? I've been to Hell!"

"This is not about you!"

Eddie threw his arms into the air. Nothing he could say was right. Nothing.

"What do you want me to say?"

"I–" Kelly stuttered, realising she didn't truly know the answer to that question. "I want you to apologise."

"For what?"

"For what you said!"

"What did I say?"

"You–" she stuttered once more, searching for the right words. "Well, I don't remember, but I still think you should apologise for it."

"Okay," he offered with a shrug of his shoulders. "I'm sorry."

"But how are you apologising when you don't even know what it's for?"

"Kelly, that's what you just told me you wanted me to do!"

"Yes, but I don't want a fake apology!"

"Then what the hell do you want?"

"I – I don't know!"

She turned and faced the window. She rested her weight on one leg, using her other foot to tap agitatedly on the floor. Her arms remained tightly folded, her lips pursed together.

After a few hesitant moments, she felt two gentle arms tucking around her waist. She went to push them away but just found them tightening their soft, heartfelt grip around her once more.

"No, Eddie."

"Kelly, we don't even know what we're fighting about."

He kissed her neck.

Damn it, she hated when he kissed her neck.

Within seconds her anger diluted. She resisted at first, adamant that she wanted to stay enraged, but his embrace was just too inviting. She sank into it, allowing him to wrap his arms around her until she was fully cocooned in his comfortable warmth.

"I know there's no way to put into words what you went through, what it was like," Eddie whispered into her ear. "I hear your screams in the night before they wake you up. The flashbacks are horrific; the things it made you do were horrible, and I think you're incredibly strong for coping as well as you have."

She couldn't help it. His words were so sincere, so inviting. She allowed them to wrap around her heart, coating it with reassurance and undeniable love.

"It kills me that I don't know what I can do about it, or how I could make it go away. There's hardly much comparison out there — there's not really any possessed-by-the-devil-anonymous groups you can go join, are there?"

She nodded. It was true.

"Just know that I will never, ever abandon you. It will never make me run away."

"You promise?"

"Of course. I would never do anything that could cause you even the slightest amount of pain."

She sank deeper into his arms, feeling comforted and reassured in a way she didn't even realise she had craved.

Three months later, he killed her.

APRIL 2003

THREE YEARS, FOUR MONTHS SINCE MILLENNIUM
NIGHT

CHAPTER TWENTY-NINE

*D*erek stood at the altar.

To think, he had once planned to stand there as a groom. Many years ago, and long faded in his memory now, was the picture of a woman. A woman he loved with every piece of him, to whom he had given a ring and made plans.

But he had given it all up. He had been young and foolish, and chose this life over her.

Eddie had once seen a photograph of her in his house, one that he had subsequently hidden.

No other mention had been made of her since the day she left.

Funny, really, how he thought of her now. Wondering where she was. Wondering if, whilst running the vacuum around the house or dropping her kids off at school, she ever thought of him. Just a passing thought, shooting by like something out the window of a train. Brief, but definite nonetheless.

He wondered if she had been granted passage to Heaven.

"Can I help you, my child?" came a softly spoken voice from behind Derek.

He quickly dunked his flask into the holy water and took

what he needed, placing it inside his jacket pocket and turning around to face the priest.

It was not a father Derek recognised. He was a short, podgy man, with a round bald spot amidst a head of messy hair. His face was red and sweaty, no doubt in fear of what was to come.

"No, thank you," Derek replied. "I have what I need."

"You were stealing the holy water," the father said gently.

"I see nothing gets past you, Father," Derek observed. "It is for a just cause, I assure you."

"I am sure it is. Bad times are coming."

"They are indeed."

In a hurry, Derek forced a smile and shuffled past the old man, but was halted by a few alarming words.

"If you are stealing holy water, it must mean you are planning to fight what is coming."

Against his better judgement, Derek turned, peering at the father. Priest or not, Derek was already tired of this conversation.

"And what if I am? What do you know of the rapture?"

"It was said it would be the second coming of Christ. That Heaven would plant him on this earth once again."

"What if I told you Heaven had planted their messiah on this earth, and he was powerful, and he could fight?"

"Then you would pique my interest."

"What if I also told you that what was coming was far too strong, even for someone conceived of Heaven, just like Jesus was? Yes, Father, I plan to fight. But I would suggest you hide, or take your ride up to Heaven."

Derek turned to leave but was stopped once more.

"Do you not have faith in God?" the father insisted. "Do you not trust that he will do good by us?"

Derek snarled. After spending so much time wanting to know why their God didn't do more, he grew livid over such a question. Blind, unaltered, unjustified faith incensed him.

It wasn't a case of believing in God.

He had a child conceived by Heaven and a fallen angel on his side. He had fought in God's name against demons of this earth for decades; that much was true.

He had faith that God was there.

But did he have faith in that God?

Faith that God would ever get off his arse and do something other than sending them a warrior in the form of a helpless boy?

God was never someone he felt he had on his side.

"No, I do not," Derek bluntly stated. "But I do have faith."

"In what?"

Derek peered at the priest, who seemed so eager to impart the apparent power of faith into Derek. So desperate to think that his words were wise and not disillusioned.

"I have faith in Eddie."

"But are you not afraid you will have to answer to God?"

Derek narrowed his eyes into a menacing, sinister glare.

"Do you know what we have had to do to represent your God? The awful, hellish things we have had to do so he can keep his hands clean?"

"My child–"

Derek took a few sinister strides toward the priest until he was inches from his face.

"I would ask God's forgiveness. But after everything, if me and him ever come face-to-face — he will have to beg for *mine*."

Derek turned and marched out of the church, ignoring further shouts and questions designed to bring him back into the pointless debate.

* * *

SURE, the father was trying to talk some sense into a disciple and do what he thought was right.

But Derek truly believed that the father was trying to convince himself more than anyone else. If he knew what the rapture meant, what it truly was in more than mere biblical terms, he would likely deny it.

Which is to be expected. Denial is the most common human trait, despite also being the most counterproductive.

Derek walked for five minutes down a few entwining paths until he met with Martin. They had decided to use the location in which the heir had risen and taunted them last time. Somewhere familiar that the antichrist would find them.

The field of death, or so it felt. Beside a swing set that Jenny saw as significant enough to use in her attempts to get through to Eddie.

She may have failed, yes — but if this was Jenny's idea then they needed to listen to her.

Failing to listen to her was what caused such a catastrophic failure before.

"Ready?" Martin prompted.

"Nearly."

The night was descending and dark-grey clouds hovered overhead. The field was deserted. Some naïve people would see this as luck; that there weren't any innocent bystanders who could get caught in the crossfire.

They knew better than that. People had an instinct for such danger, even if they didn't know or acknowledge it.

Derek took his leather bag and made his way to the swing set. The place Eddie and Jenny had grown up. The place they had become such close friends, where they had comforted and consoled each other through difficult times.

It was rusted. Left to rot by a neglectful council who didn't care for the sentimentality associated with such landmarks.

He knelt down and opened his bag. A puff of dust rose like smoke, and Derek resisted the urge to choke.

He withdrew the items. Items he had used long ago. Back

before Eddie became so prolific at this activity that Derek's own abilities at performing an exorcism had grown redundant.

He withdrew each item with care, raising it to his forehead and closing his eyes for a short moment; before placing it gently and precisely on the floor before him.

A cross. Wooden, with a splintered edge. Old but sturdy, with the faded bumps of a crucified Jesus fixed upon it.

A flask of holy water with the cross marked upon it, taken from the church hours ago.

A Bible. Leather bound, with faded brown pages and illegibly small writing. Part of it was in Latin. It had been a while since he had used the dated language, but he was ready to call on his old knowledge should the process require him to.

Rosary beads, which he did not place carefully with his other items, but instead kissed and placed around his neck, tucking them under his shirt.

And finally, he withdrew salt. He poured a small handful in his palm, which he then poured in a circle around himself.

He bowed his head. Closed his eyes.

"Eddie, have mercy. God, the Son, please give him safe passage in this merciless time."

His eyes welled up. He fought against it. Now was not the time. Now was the fight of his life.

This was it.

Either Eddie was out there, somewhere, able to fight his way back.

Or...

Or... the world ends tonight.

Derek rose to his feet. He took the cross firmly in his left hand. He placed the holy water in his pocket and held the Bible in his right.

"Right you prick," he muttered. "Where are you?"

"But about that day or hour no one knows, not even the angels in heaven, nor the Son, but only the Father."

Mark 13:32

CHAPTER THIRTY

*T*hunder rumbled ever closer with a threatening familiarity, but it did nothing to intimidate Martin or Derek.

They had far more to worry about than the weather.

A trickle of rain pattered against the empty earth. Grey clouds blocked the moon until flickering lamplight was the only illumination available, casting a faint amber glow that deflected off the rusted metal of the park.

"Martin," Derek prompted. "It's time."

"Where's Cassy?" Martin asked, looking around. "She was supposed to be here."

"We can't wait any longer. She will get here, trust me."

Martin stood forward, taking in a deep breath. It was a strange feeling, knowing that you could well be dead within minutes. Knowing that everything you have done could be rendered meaningless.

Not just his preparation for this war.

The failed parents' evening reports. The feeding of his disabled mother. The arguments, the tantrums, the fallouts, the girls, the friends, the bullies — everything could mean nothing.

History was not written by those who lose.

He would not be remembered for failing. His name would not go down in history in a world ravaged by demons and death.

This was his immortality.

He had no army. He just had two faithful followers who had never faltered in their belief in him, despite such blatant, undeniable evidence that he was not strong enough.

It was time to repay their faith in him.

It was time to forget all those pointless things in life.

Those teachers can tell his parents he's a lazy little shit. Fine. Who cares?

Those bullies can tell him he won't amount to anything. Where are they now?

Those girls can laugh. Those friends can run. The shouting can get louder and it won't mean a damn thing.

Because this was it.

This is what will define me.

"All right, you fucker!" Martin screamed out, hoping his taunt would be heard. "Come on then! Time for round two!"

He waited, allowing the rain to seep through his t-shirt and drench his skinny body.

"Come on, where are you?"

A figure appeared in the distance. Walking closer, a limping silhouette.

Martin glanced over his shoulder at Derek, who looked equally perplexed, also peering to see who it was.

Martin watched as this figure fell to its knees and clambered back up again. Something was attached to it. Something long and heavy.

It was Cassy.

As she grew closer, her face grew clearer.

But despite her inherent angelic grace, her face was bloodied. Mangled. Distorted. She was hurt.

"Cassy?" Martin shouted. He went to march forward, but a shout from Derek behind him kept him rooted to the spot.

"Don't, Martin – wait."

Cassy stumbled closer and, as she did, her body faded into view. It was wrapped in chains. Big, metallic chains entwined around her chest again and again, with a longer chain leading into the darkness behind her.

"Oh my God, what happened?" Martin asked. Ignoring Derek's shout, he ran forward.

"Don't!" Cassy screamed, forcing Martin to stumble to a sudden stop. "It's a trap!"

Martin frowned. A trap?

Surely if he was to fight this thing, there would be no traps?

He was ready to fight.

Straightening himself up, he sauntered forward with an air of arrogance, ready for this so-called trap.

A slow growl rumbled across the air, shaking the confidence he had mustered.

"Where is he?" Martin demanded, doing all he could to sound strong.

"He's–" Cassy began, but before she could complete her sentence she went flying backwards, back into the cloak of darkness, encompassed in the shadows behind her.

Martin didn't move. He watched, waiting for the next taunt, or the next attack. Waiting warily for the next move.

Staring cautiously into pitch-black. Just waiting for whatever was there to appear.

He looked to Derek, who was the same; poised, still, wary.

The ground rumbled, trembling under a few thudding footsteps. A huge banging became louder, growing closer.

Then, from the shadows, it emerged.

The large beast with hooves, claws, fangs, razor-sharp spikes, and red demented eyes.

In the heir's hand was Cassy, held tightly by a claw that could crush her without any effort.

"Let her go!" Martin demanded.

Dripping blood and saliva, the heir's mouth curved into an open grin, a few hearty chuckles booming out.

"You've gotten cocky," the heir declared.

"Let. Her. Go!"

"Finally!" the heir sighed. "Enough of this waiting. Let's get your death out of the way."

CHAPTER THIRTY-ONE

*E*ddie thudded to the floor like his body was made of weights. His chest felt like it was going to burst. His head pounded, beating against the skull he knew wasn't even there.

He willed himself out of it. Told himself to endure the pain. It wasn't real.

He felt such agony when the heir was on Earth. And, if the heir was on Earth, Eddie knew bad things were happening.

He could feel everything. This was the piece of Hell he was attached to. The link the devil couldn't sever.

If he was the heir, he could see through his eyes. See what he was doing.

Only…

Did he really want to see that? Did he want to see the death and destruction being caused by… him?

He couldn't deny that anymore.

It was being done by him.

Just, not the part with the soul attached.

Yes.

He reluctantly bowed his head.

I'm going to have to see this.

He closed his eyes, allowing himself to sink. Sink out of his mind, out of his body, further into the vile casing of the heir. Allowing himself to see through the eyes of...

It was easier than he thought.

He was staring through the heir's eyes within seconds. Feeling his stretched flesh encase his bones.

He was relieved that it worked.

That was, until he saw the scene in front of him.

Oh, God.

He felt something in his hand. Except, it wasn't a hand. It was bigger than that. It was a claw. With sharp nails and...

Cassy.

His own sister.

An angel. Being disgraced, used as a taunt. A bloody, bruised face.

He waved Cassy back and forth in his hand, pulling on a chain in the other, a chain that led back to her. She was wrapped in restraints. And she was crying.

She was begging.

But not with Eddie. She was begging with something else.

With the boy in front of him.

Martin. The piece of Heaven. The biblical piece of the rapture — this boy was the second coming of Christ. This was a child conceived by Heaven, just as had happened two thousand years before.

The only hope humans had.

And Cassy was begging him. Begging him to do nothing. Not to accept the taunt. To let her die, to let her be shattered into thousands of pieces of bright light that would shine down on them like stars — as Eddie always imagined a murdered angel's fate would be.

Except no angel had ever died before. They had fallen, but this could be the first...

Which, in that case, made it undeniable — they truly were losing.

Martin's faced moulded into a snarl. Full of hatred against this thing before him.

Eddie didn't want to look, but he had to.

He had to.

Because there he was, beyond Martin. The only man who had ever believed in Eddie.

Derek.

About to help fight him to the death. To be the last stand between Heaven and Hell.

To be the last person fighting Eddie, the man he had helped create.

Eddie fell out of the heir's eyes, out of the heir's body, falling back onto the solid ground of his cell. He couldn't take it anymore. It was too tough.

Derek. The man who had trained him.

Now trying to kill him.

Except, he wasn't.

Martin was the one fighting. Derek was further back. What was he doing?

Eddie leapt back to life, diving into the heir's eyes once more.

Derek had items. What were they?

Eddie peered into the distance.

A cross. Holy water. A Bible.

Those were items used in an exorcism.

Why has he got items for an exorcism...?

It struck him, in a gratifying moment of realisation. Derek hadn't given up on him.

He was trying to get to Eddie. He was trying to remove the soul, save him from where he was trapped, bring him back.

Oh God, Derek.

Derek did still believe in him.

But... how? How could Derek do that?

There was no way out.

Then he heard Derek's voice. So faint that if he even moved he wouldn't have been able to hear it.

"Eddie, have mercy. God, the Son, please give him safe passage in this merciless time."

"Derek..."

Eddie held his position behind the monster's eyes. The position where he planned to stay. He felt physically closer to Derek there — maybe that was where he needed to be to give the exorcism the best chance of working?

He felt invigorated. A new lease on life, a spurt of energy firing through him like a jolt of electricity.

If he could see through the heir of Hell's eyes... Then surely... Surely...

Could he do more than just see?

Could he alter the heir's actions? Even take over completely?

After all, it was him. He was seeing through his own eyes, it was the body he belonged to.

He clenched his fists. Held his arms out in the position of the beast, tried to move them, put all his energy into it, urging himself on, willing himself to do it.

But it was no good.

The claw tightened around Cassy and he felt there was nothing he could do.

CHAPTER THIRTY-TWO

*M*artin whipped his hands around in circles, furiously beating the air until flickers of gold began to generate.

Time to be brave, Martin.

No time for being young, or doubting his convictions. The plan had been made, and it was time to execute it.

Focus, Martin. Fuck everything else, just focus.

The heir of Hell's glare intensified. It appeared amused yet angry. Amused that Martin thought he could oppose it, and angry that Martin even dared.

"Just kill it!" Cassy insisted. "Ignore me!"

The heir's grip tightened around Cassy's chest, squeezing her into silence and submission.

Martin concentrated on his surroundings, listening to the thunder, taking in the smell of fine rain. He closed his eyes, silencing his thoughts. Focussing on nothing but what was around him.

His eyes shot open. He harnessed a large string of fire in his hands, turning it into a sharp point. He threw it out, landing it on the heir's wrist, forcing it to drop Cassy to the ground.

Cassy stumbled onto her front, then launched herself forward. She ran messily back and forth, trying to retain her balance, and get away from the heir.

Martin retracted his fiery whip and slid it down the back of her chains. She collapsed to the ground once more, wriggling herself out of her incarceration.

The heir snarled. It grew so livid that its body set on fire, flames running down its spine to accompany its aggressive snarl.

It ignored Cassy, who continued to run into the distance, peeling off her chains — choosing to focus on the impudent boy before him.

Martin went to throw a whip of fire. He felt a brief glow of smugness from the impact of his burning blade, but found his optimism fading as the heir whacked the fire away.

Its feet beat against the floor as it edged its way forward with large, sinister strides. The simmer of an earthquake followed every placement of its foot. It swiped its sharp claw toward Martin, who conjured a gust of wind just in time to surge himself upwards and out of the way.

He fell onto his back, leaving himself exposed.

The heir curled its claw into a tight fist and sent it soaring downwards into the soggy grass. Martin rolled just in time to narrowly miss the strike, feeling the large gust brush against him as the heir retracted its bulky claw.

Martin stared up at the heir, awaiting its next move. The heir lurched forward, glaring, ready for its lethal strike.

"You cannot prevent what's coming!" it screeched with such volume a nearby lamppost waved.

Martin crawled backwards, trying to get to his feet.

The heir sent its fist into the ground, shaking the surface with such ferocity it sent Martin flailing into the air and back onto his front.

"You don't get it, do you…"

Martin crawled forward, trying to get to his knees, but another slam sent him rolling across the floor.

He stumbled to his feet and turned away from the heir, sprinting for his life.

He was running away.

Why am I running away?

"I killed Kelly to complete my ascension," the heir reminded Martin.

Martin turned over his shoulder, willing himself to be brave, searching for a way to fight this. But the heir was lifting its claws, storming forward, a rumbling earthquake with each step.

It was chasing him.

And Martin abruptly realised why he was running away.

I can't fight this. It's too strong.

"I killed Jenny to show you that fighting was futile."

Martin tumbled to his side, falling from the shake of the earth's vibrations.

In the distance he saw Derek praying, Cassy diving to his side, joining in.

Another slam into the surface and Martin bounced up and down, landing on his arm with a painful howl.

He had no more spells. No more elements he could manipulate.

Fire. Wind. That was it. That was all he had mastered.

Only then did it strike him how ill-prepared he was.

It was a ridiculous thought, really.

I wasn't ever going to be able to defeat the heir.

"Now I will kill you to end the world."

The claw of this creature slammed over him, trapping him like a cage. He tried to find a gap in its claws that he thought he could crawl through, but he couldn't. He was stuck. Stuck inside the sharp claws of the heir of Hell.

He conjured a ball of fire and sent it into the claw.

It flinched.

But it did not falter.

The claw wrapped itself around Martin and scooped him up like he was a plate of food.

As he was swept through the air he felt the claw tighten, gripping, constricting his chest. He gasped for oxygen, helplessly punching the thick hand wrapped around him.

He was held before the heir's face, made to look into the heir's demonic, bloody eyes.

The grip tightened and tightened.

It suffocated him until he couldn't breathe. He felt his insides squeeze, his muscles compress, his bones crush.

This was it.

This was his resistance.

CHAPTER THIRTY-THREE

*T*he sides of the wooden cross indented into Derek's hand, such was the tightness of his grip.

He watched in horror as the heir wrapped its sharp, curved claws around Martin's body and squeezed, pressing all the oxygen out of his lungs.

Derek needed to do something. He needed to do it quickly.

But what?

He had no powers. Martin was the one who had the gift he was supposed to be using it to defeat this thing. That gift was already proving to be insignificant.

Derek felt Cassy's weak hand on his shoulder. He turned around to see her wounded expression.

"What can I do?" Derek asked.

"Your gift," Cassy reminded him.

"I have no gift. Eddie and Martin were the ones with the gift, not me."

"That's not true." She knelt beside him and peered intently into his eyes. "Perform the exorcism. Call on Eddie. Do it now."

Derek bowed his head. They were supposed to have the heir restrained, kept bound whilst he performed the rite of exorcism. To do it whilst the beast was still thrashing around would be near impossible.

If the heir saw Derek performing the exorcism without being restrained, it would kill him in an instant.

But he had no choice.

Clutching the cross, gripping the Bible, he leapt to his feet and marched forward. Marched toward the beast that was slowly killing Martin.

"From all evil, deliver us, oh Lord," he began. "Deliver us, oh *Eddie!*"

The beast roared.

Martin's eyelids flickered heavily. His face grew pale, his arms punching with less and less ferocity.

They were losing him.

"Hear us, Eddie. From all sin, from wrath, from sudden and provided death, hear us."

He held his cross out, pointing it directly at the monster that consumed Derek in shadows.

"Hold on, Martin!" Derek cried out.

Martin tried to shout back but couldn't. His eyes were distant, staying shut longer on each heavy blink. Derek could see the fading fight on Martin's face. He endeavoured to stay conscious, to keep battling; but he was losing life, and Derek needed to act.

Derek needed Eddie to act.

"Hear us, Edward King. From the snares of the devil, from anger, hatred, and all ill will, from lightning and tempest — hear us, *Edward King!*"

The rain mixed with his perspiration, dripping down his face, but he didn't feel a drop of it.

Derek glanced over his shoulder.

Cassy stood a few yards behind him. Nodding reassuringly.

"All holy saints, pass our message on," Derek spoke.

"Deliver us, Edward King," Cassy echoed behind him.

The heir turned its glare toward them.

But Martin no longer fought. His head slanted to the side, his eyes opening and closing groggily.

Derek's eyes faltered, fighting tears, as he saw Martin seconds away from death.

"Be merciful, deliver us."

"Deliver us, Edward King."

"Hear us, Eddie, for all the good in this world, hear us!"

"Hear us, Edward King."

The beast froze momentarily.

Hovered vacantly.

Loosened its grip.

Derek turned to Cassy, who was equally confused, then turned back to the fading face of the heir.

Derek was sure he saw a glint of an old friend in the monster's eyes.

CHAPTER THIRTY-FOUR

*E*ddie could feel the heir's anger bursting through him, surging through his body, filling his veins with gushing blood of hate.

Every part of him was consumed with this urge for destruction. The desire to kill, maim, and torture his way to annihilation. To reach out and suffocate, to rip apart anyone or anything that opposed him.

Through the heir's eyes, he could see Derek. Marching toward him, crucifix in hand.

"No…" whimpered Eddie. "Please, Derek, I'll kill you…"

He felt his right hand tighten, grip around something bumpy. He turned and looked.

Martin.

The young man thrashed out at his claws, but it just felt like a twitch or a tinge of discomfort. After a few seconds, he didn't even feel the slight discomfort anymore. The boy grew pale, his fighting growing less and less.

Eddie was killing him.

He could feel it. The life rushing away from Heaven's saviour. The second coming being crushed into submission.

His hand tightened around Martin's chest, constricting his breathing with ease.

Martin's fighting grew weaker.

The thrashing turned to stumbling punches, to light taps.

Martin's eyes closed and his head tilted.

Then Eddie heard something. Something he wasn't expecting to hear.

"From the snares of the devil, from anger, from hatred," Derek spoke, staring the heir straight in the eyes, "and all ill will from lightning and tempest — hear us, Edward King!"

His name.

Derek had said his name.

Derek... Oh dear God...

What was Derek doing?

Then, with stark realisation, Eddie realised.

They knew he was there. They knew Eddie was still there, behind the eyes of the heir of Hell. They were trying to get to him, to his trapped soul, trying to free it from its capture. To bring him back into the heir's body.

"All holy saints, pass our message on," Derek continued.

"Deliver us, Edward King."

A soft, angelic voice.

It was Cassy. She was okay.

It's you... My God...

She stood behind Derek, her body hanging weakly, obviously wounded — but alive.

"Cassy…" Eddie whimpered.

He needed to do something. He needed to repay their faith, to find a way back, to do something rather than just watching through the eyes of the devil's servant.

But what?

What could he do?

"Be merciful, deliver us."

"Deliver us, Edward King."

His name.

Cassy was saying his name. Derek was saying his name.

They were doing their part, he had to do his.

He racked his brain. What could he do?

The heir.

Surely, if he could see through the heir's eyes, he could seep into other parts of him? He could feel Martin's body growing limp in his hand. If he could feel it, could he control it?

"Hear us, Eddie, for all the good in this world, hear us!"

"Hear us, Edward King!"

Martin was going to die.

If the heir did not stop squeezing, Martin would be dead in seconds.

It had been a while, but Eddie remembered what he had to do to conjure the elements. To throw fire like he had at the devil to rescue Derek from Hell.

It all felt so long ago.

He had to concentrate. Feel. Listen to every sense.

So that's what he did.

He listened. Rain. A pattering of rain with a distant thunder. Every bit of it striking his skin.

His skin. Growing wet. Feeling Martin's body within his tight clutches.

He could smell the rain. See his former mentor and angelic sister willing him to come forth.

He could feel hatred. Nothing but hatred. Surging through him.

And Martin, tight in his hands.

He gripped Martin with the heir, gripping tightly. Did what the heir was doing, so that they became one.

Then he loosened his grip.

He felt the heir's hand twitch. The heir was trying to resist.

Eddie had to concentrate.

The rain. The thunder. Derek. Cassy.

He opened his palm.

Opened it and felt Martin slide out of it.

He looked to Derek.

A glint in Derek's thankful eyes showed a hint of recognition. That Derek could see Eddie in there. That Derek recognised his old friend.

Eddie lifted the heir's arms out to the side.

He held them rigidly, resisting the fight the heir was putting up.

His arms shook, but Eddie was in control.

"Do it, Derek," he spoke. "Do it now."

CHAPTER THIRTY-FIVE

*M*artin fell to the ground with a thud and rolled onto his back.

He wheezed, gasping for air. His muscles shook. His bones felt like jelly, wobbling under the weight of himself. He struggled to get to his knees.

Cassy was at his side. He had no idea when she got there; he hadn't seen her approach, but she was there, her arm around him.

"Just wait, Martin," Cassy said. "You may have a concussion. Let yourself regain your strength."

"But the heir–"

"You'll be all right for a moment."

Martin turned his head toward Derek, who stood defiantly before the heir, a cross held out in his hands.

The heir stood stiffly, with its arms held out to the side like a crucifix. There was something different about its eyes, something different about its expression.

It looked… sincere.

Its arms didn't move. They were held rigidly to its side, the palms open, vibrating under invisible pressure.

"Do it," came a voice from the heir. It was a voice that did not match the face; it sounded more human. "Do it now!"

Martin looked to Cassy, full of confusion.

"Whose voice is that?" he inquired.

Cassy smiled.

"Eddie," she answered. "That's Eddie's voice."

Martin couldn't believe it.

"Martin, we need you!" Derek said. "We need your restraint spell, now!"

The rigid arms of the heir shook as if under an immense pressure, struggling to remain still.

It's Eddie... He's doing this...

Cassy helped Martin to his feet and he regained his balance.

Holy crap, this could work...

Martin stood firmly with his feet shoulder-width apart, glaring at the demon, glaring with an intensity the captive monster could not match.

He lifted his right hand out. He rotated it in a small circle, slowly growing bigger and bigger, extending the radius of his finger's movement.

Sure enough, a gold circle flickered before him, taking form, growing larger and larger.

Martin held his hands out to steady the circle, willing any flickers or breaks to disappear.

The golden circle grew solid.

He threw his hands out, throwing the circle forward until it latched around the demon's body, entwining it in a forced embrace.

The restraint tightened around the heir, forcing him into submission. Martin squeezed the circle, gripping it like an enchanted lasso.

Martin fell onto his back. What little energy he had had been expended. He collapsed into a heap, his head hitting the ground.

Cassy put her arms around him.

"Did I do it?" Martin asked between gasps for air.

"Yes, Martin," Cassy answered. "Of course you did."

Martin rolled onto his back.

His eyes searched for Derek, who stared smugly back at him.

His eyes then searched for the heir, who hovered mid-air with a tight, gold circle gripping around its chest, holding securely in place.

Martin had done it.

Derek could perform the exorcism.

Eddie was in there somewhere, they knew it. They had seen it.

CHAPTER THIRTY-SIX

*N*ever mind the damp, the cold, or the bindings around his chest. Nor the knowledge that he was no closer to a throne in Hell than he was escaping from his incarceration.

Never mind the starvation, the thirst, or the desperate longing to see light.

It was the incessant, faraway drip that was making Bandile's mind spin into madness.

For as long as he had been there, an undetected dribble of water had been trickling from an unidentifiable location, a tediously repetitive soundtrack to his restricted movements.

He had no idea how long it had been.

Days, maybe.

Or hours that seemed like days.

He had been fed a few pieces of bread and allowed a sip of water — all before they had marched off to what Bandile presumed was their battle with the heir of Hell. Their battle to bring back Edward King's soul.

Then they would collect Bandile.

Take him to the battle-ground.

Tell him to place his hand on the soul and use his Satanist values and devil-worshipping history to allow this soul to retake the form of the one they so proudly call Eddie.

He was going to do no such thing.

He struggled against the ropes, pushing at them, feeding his hand through a crack.

Then, to his astonishment, his hand seeped through. He felt it flap freely in the moist air of the room.

Then it struck him.

His plan was to refuse to turn their saviour from a ball of elements to its human casing.

But what if he did more…

What if he could get free…

Then, when Martin came to fetch him…

He could kill the boy, as he had originally intended.

That would be a far better plan.

Reaching his hand upwards, straining his wrist, he grabbed the rope, squeezing it tightly, gripping his hand fully around its thick, chafing surface.

He pulled on it.

It was too tight, too secure for it to budge.

But it wouldn't be if he kept tugging.

And, as far as he was concerned, he had all the time in the world.

So he tugged some more. Pulled on it, lifted his hand behind the rope, twisting his wrist painfully, and pushing from underneath it.

It loosened. Although fractionally, the rope still loosened.

He had a chance.

If he kept doing this, he could get free.

If they came to find him before he managed, then fine, he could just refuse to turn the soul to human.

But if he could do it before they came…

If he could be free when Martin arrived…

He could kill him.

End it.

Earn my place at the devil's side.

With a wide grin he formulated his plan, running his options through his mind.

He pulled and pulled at the rope, gradually loosening it, imagining the cold body of Martin beneath his hands.

CHAPTER THIRTY-SEVEN

*T*here is no fury like a devil's wrath.

The god of the underworld, the ultimate fallen angel, the sick and twisted being of torture and death.

When you piss him off, you piss off Hell.

He detested the three puny, pathetic creatures who dared oppose him. The same insufferable humans who'd mustered pitiful attempts against him for years. Those who were ensnaring his heir to reach through to the soul of Edward King.

The soul was trapped in a room that could not be escaped from, guarded by the strongest guard of Hell, Geryon.

But this did not dull the devil's rage.

"Enough!" he declared, sat lavishly upon his throne of skulls with flames firing from his body and scorching the black air. "Enough of waiting. It's time."

This was more than a rapture. The rapture had been and gone. The second coming had been attempted, and it had proven unworthy of his antichrist.

Heaven had had its time ruling over the mortal world. Their time was over.

This was the moment he had been waiting for.

The apocalypse of man. The scourge of pitiful, frail humans. It was time to rid them from the world.

It would be a canal feast for his minions of Hell.

With an infuriated, hostile nod to his subordinates, he indicated it was time.

Demons gathered at the gates of Hell, bouncing with excitement, salivating at the prospect of a buffet of humanity. And, with a grand swing, the gates were opened for the first time in an eternity.

The demons hastily climbed up the entwining roots of Earth, soaring upwards, making their way from the fiery core to the surface where the humans dwelled, living out their pitiful lives while waiting for death.

The worthy had gone to Heaven. It was time to cull the rest.

Demon after demon emerged, furious, ready for revenge. Bouncing onto the Earth in various locations, devouring the helpless fools that stood in their way.

Whilst many demons plunged themselves forward, the devil's closest disciple took its time climbing upwards and surveying the world before him.

This was a demon with a specific target in mind.

This was the prince of Hell.

Balam.

This demon had been defeated on millennium night, removed from the body of Adeline by the clutches of the mortal form of Edward King. This man had freed the soul of the heir's sister so she could pass on to Heaven, the place of her conception.

The memory made him sick. Made him swelter with rage.

But Edward King hadn't known who Edward King was, or who he would really become.

Millennium night had been when the heir had risen — only, it hadn't emerged in the instant it rose. It had taken years for the Hell within Edward King to surface and complete the Devil's Three, but Balam had been there; Balam had witnessed it.

Balam had been there on millennium night. Although Edward King had banished him back to Hell, he had no doubt detected the coming of Hell's spawn.

Now was the time he could take back Cassy King for his own.

An angel.

Pah!

There was no agreement anymore. No truce between Heaven and Hell.

No reason why she should not die and be plunged back into the pits of Hell where Balam could finish her off.

He struck a hefty fist through the thick cement, the barrier humans thought would sever their ties between their road and the soil beneath. Balam broke through the cement like it was a weak piece of bread, sending a crack down the centre of a busy road, splitting it in two, sending cars and buildings into chaos.

He stepped forward, scowling at those who did not abruptly part out of his way. Cars screeched to a halt, except for one that sped up. Balam reached his fist out and slammed it into the bonnet of the vehicle, punching straight through, shattering it to pieces.

All around him were lights. Images of lights, busy streets, people swarming around him.

These people screamed and ran.

His human head scowled at their cowardice. His other two heads — one of a bull and one of a ram – peered around at the opportunities for death and destruction. The bull head snorted as the ram head grinned.

His flaming serpent's tail thwacked against a nearby building, smashing windows and collapsing the brick wall. He grinned mercilessly as people dove out the of building, desperately leaping to their salvation. With a grand swipe of his tail, he lunged any remains of this building into the crack in the ground, sending them sailing, hundreds of lives screaming into the pits of Hell.

His faithful bear dove out of the pits, landing at his feet and he mounted it, ready to travel.

He reached his arm out and grabbed a human by the neck, lifting it up to face his eyes, laughing at the intolerable weakness of its weeping face.

"Where am I?" roared Balam.

"T – T – Tokyo!" cried the human.

Balam gripped the human's neck tighter, snapping its head off like a twig.

His bear galloped, taking Balam into the air, onwards to his destination.

Toward the United Kingdom, where Cassy dwelled and fought, protected by her two feeble little friends.

All around the world, similar scenes of chaos descended upon man.

In Hungary the ground opened, swallowing green countryside, turning it to flames.

The perfectly curved body of a demon sprang up; a vile, scaly woman with her mouth covered by a piece of cloth, a spike running down her spine that met a large tail whipping balls of fire back and forth. Tezrian, the goddess of war, surveyed its locale with eyes determined to ensure conflict ensued in her wake.

Umtata, South Africa. A small field full of huts.

The son of Bandile Thato dropped to his knees and prayed as he gawked at the indistinguishable face of Vetis, the tempter of the holy.

Vetis' body was brown like wood, with a white beard beneath a long, distorted face, and a grey mullet behind large antlers. Its tail whipped and thrashed, destroying lives with an instant scrape of its sharp point. It flew over Thato, its large wings beating against the wind.

The tempter of the holy had already done its job with the child's father. Now it needed to find more innocents, forcing them to deal pain upon those they love.

Across the world, demon after demon descended.

Horns, antlers, whipping sharp tails, fierce claws, and red, fiery eyes.

The cities turned to splattered locations of death. The countryside stained with blood. The smell of fire and rotting hung on the air.

Masses of demons, hordes of monsters, all with one thing on their mind.

CHAPTER THIRTY-EIGHT

*D*erek held the cross out like a sword, directing it at the heir, who hovered helplessly before him.

The heir's eyes were full of malice. Angry snarls as it writhed and struggled against the restraints. Its claws kept retracting and opening again, wanting to be used, wanting to serve a lethal blow as punishment for daring to do this.

Derek knew this spell wouldn't hold him.

He knew it was only managing because of Eddie.

And when the spell broke, the heir's temper would not be easily contained.

He had to be fast. He had to concentrate, to do what he could.

Exorcisms on weak demons could last hours, days, even weeks.

This was an exorcism on the most powerful demon to have ever existed, and it had to be done in minutes.

But Derek hadn't time to consider the odds.

Besides, Eddie had found the power to exorcise a demon in far shorter periods of time. If he was battling from his end, Derek knew that they stood a chance.

If only a small one.

"From all evil deliver us, Edward King."

"Deliver us, Edward King," Cassy echoed, nudging Martin to join them.

"From all sin, from all wrath, from sudden and unprovided death, deliver us."

"Deliver us, Edward King!" Cassy shouted, Martin joining her.

Come on, Eddie.

The demon's anger subsided momentarily, turning into mocking disdain. It chuckled in a pitch so deep it made the ground rumble. Its mouth grew into an infuriating grin.

"What does it say," it boomed, "when you no longer pray to your God, but to a weak man conceived by Hell?"

"Eddie is not weak!" Martin cried out.

"Martin," Cassy interrupted, placing a calming hand on his shoulder. "During an exorcism, a demon will always try to say things to taunt you. You have to ignore what it says."

"By the mystery of your incantation," Derek persevered. "By your passion, by your holy presence on this earth, by your own history of fighting Hell's creatures, hear me!"

"Deliver us, Edward King."

The demon's low chuckle grew to roaring hysterics. Its laughter shook them, its breath exhaling so forcefully its snorts blew them back with a savage gust of wind.

"You are praying for the soul of a dead man! *I am Edward King!*"

Derek narrowed his eyes.

He must resist the taunts.

This thing was *not* Eddie.

This thing could *never* be Eddie.

It was a vile, monstrous expeditor of Hell.

Sure, that may have been what Eddie was conceived to be.

But he had faith in him.

He had to keep faith in Eddie.

Or this would be for nothing.

"By your death and burial!"

"Your death and burial will be following soon…"

"Your Advocate on the day of judgement!"

"I can feel this getting looser… Edward King can't help you anymore…"

"On this, the day of rapture, bring back your faithful soul and rid us of this foul, disgusting beast!"

"Deliver us, Edward King!"

Sparks ignited off the restraints. Fragments began to crumble. Holes appeared.

Martin stood to cast another restraint spell, but the heir managed to loosen a claw that it used to send Martin flying onto his back.

Cassy rushed to his side.

"That you spare us, that your pardon us, that you bring us to your true penance I tell you, Edward King, you can do this. Bring forth your soul and send this creature back to Hell!"

"Deliver us, Edward King."

The muscles of the demon clenched, growing larger, bursting against the golden restraint, causing it to flicker and break in more and more places.

"I'm not alone, you know…" the demon announced, sniffing something in the air, like he could sense something.

Derek withdrew his holy water and threw a handful onto the heir's foot.

It tinged with a small puff of smoke. The heir just sneered cockily, continuing to push against its imprisonment.

"You restore my unity, my faith in what is good," Derek continued.

The demon lifted its jaw and grabbed part of the restraints with its fanged teeth, ripping it away like a piece of meat and throwing it to ash upon the ground.

"Lead all the non-believers in your wake."

A large hole grew in the remains of the spell's binding and it fell.

"That you confirm and preserve us, judge us, help us — listen to us, Eddie! You are strong! *Bring yourself forth and rid us of this bastard!*"

"Deliver us, oh Edward King!"

"Come, Eddie, bring yourself to this unholy world and fight by our sides — we compel you, *deliver us!*"

"Deliver us, Edward King!"

Ash crumpled into a black sooty mound by the heir's feet.

Free at last its face rose, looking ahead with furious vengeance.

CHAPTER THIRTY-NINE

Wheezing and coughing, Martin rose to his feet. Cassy tried to keep him down but he shook her helpful hands off.

"Derek needs my help!" he hastily observed.

"We need you alive, Martin," Cassy insisted.

"Alive for what? This is it! This is the closest we have come; this is our chance."

The heir had broken out of its restraints. As it did, it lifted its wild head to the sky and let out a tumultuous roar. It brought its heavy head down, glaring at Derek, who continued to stand before him, screaming the rites of exorcism, bellowing and bellowing his prayers to Eddie.

"Eddie, we beseech you, we need you now!"

Martin focussed.

The sound.

The smell.

The rain.

The tired muscles in his legs.

The pounding headache thumping against his skull.

Fuck it all.

The heir lifted its claw to swipe at Derek.

"No!"

Martin threw out a surge of wind that sent Derek sailing across the field, out of the heir's reach.

The heir turned its angry visage toward Martin, snarling at the impudence.

In the distance, Martin saw Derek get back to his feet and give Martin a gentle nod of thanks before continuing with his prayers.

"Yeah, and what?" Martin taunted, lifting his arms out.

He cast his mind back to the time his mate Simon kicked his arse. The time Kristy laughed at him, a girl he fancied so much, a girl he was so blindly falling in love with.

That humiliation he felt.

Never again.

This thing would not humiliate him.

No one will.

He lunged his open palms forward, conjuring a streak of fire.

But the fire hit the heir's chest and rebounded into nothing. If anything, the heir liked it. It had been spawned from a place of fire.It was like petrol to it. It kept it going.

But Martin wasn't ready to give in yet.

With his right hand, he twisted rapid circular motions, creating balls of water. After every few motions he lunged his palm forward, sending another ball of water toward the heir. With his left, he continued to fire flames.

The heir stepped forward with ease, fending these attacks off with simple waves of its claws.

Then a circle of wind encapsulated the heir, frantically spinning like a manic tornado.

"Deliver our souls and the souls of our brethren from ever-lasting damnation!" Derek persisted.

"Deliver us, Edward King!" Martin heard Cassy's voice from somewhere behind him and instantly joined in.

Derek stood behind the heir, cross in hand, sneer on his face.

The heir went to take a stride toward Derek but found itself struggling, its legs moving like they were wading through water.

Martin's jaw dropped.

It's working... The exorcism is working...

"Grant eternal rest to those departed, and eternal help to those that remain. We beseech you to come and fill this demon with your love and care."

Derek, you're a genius...

Vast circles of wind circled the heir, wrapping around it, tightening it in a tornado it couldn't brush away.

"Deliver us, Edward King!"

The demon tried to move, tried to wave the circling hurricane off him.

But something was doing this.

Someone.

The heir's immobility. Its lack of ability to resist. The turgid movement of its arms unable wipe away the fight.

It was Eddie.

Eddie was in there somewhere.

And he was fighting, just as they were.

CHAPTER FORTY

*E*ddie stiffly held his arms by his side. He could feel them shaking, the heir trying to move them, trying to resist Eddie.

But Eddie grew stronger.

Derek was doing that for him. His faith, his prayers, his reaching out to Eddie was doing all it could to force Eddie into the heir's unconscious.

But Eddie's control of this thing was still only loose, with occasional spurts of dominance. He needed to return to Earth, to find a way back to the battlefield. That was the only way.

The heir would not be able to defeat its own soul. It would face its own power, and surely be outmatched.

Yet, the more Derek spoke, the stronger he felt himself getting.

The more he was in control.

The more he grew angry.

Angry at what the heir had done, angry at the use of Eddie's face, angry at the claim that they were part of the same thing.

Eddie was in control now.

And he was furious. Rabid with anger. Drooling with a desire to kill this bastard beast that had taken over his life.

He was the master of this creature. And he was ready to unleash his fury.

Then he saw it.

Something in the sky. Something flapping, something way off.

He stepped out of the heir's body and peered upwards, above the sky of his cell.

A creature.

Eddie jumped onto the stone wall, digging his fingers into the cracks.

The wall didn't stop him. There were no rejections, nothing causing him pain like when he had tried before.

How am I doing this...

He leapt to the adjacent wall, climbing up another few stones.

Eddie took a gasp of relief. His salvation. His way out.

Something had repelled him off the stones when he had originally tried, but now...

His optimism was short-lived.

A fiery fist landed on his chest and sent him hurtling back across the room.

He looked up and saw what had just punched him, denying his escape. A demon. An atrociously vile demon. The middle of its three human heads had a large spike mounted to its centre. Its large wings ended in sharp claws, and its muscular torso descended into a large, snake-like tail with spikes decorating the entirety of its side.

"Who are you?" Eddie demanded, willing confidence to his shaky voice.

"I am Geryon, guardian of Hell." It smirked.

A guard of Hell. Sent to guard Edward King's soul.

This only confirmed to Eddie how much damage he could

do if only he could free himself from this room. They didn't send the most powerful guard of Hell to keep him trapped for nothing.

Eddie stood and ran forward, charging the demon, surging toward him, firing ahead with every piece of strength he could muster.

Geryon forced Eddie onto his back with the swipe of its tail. Though he had nothing to bleed and nothing to injure, the lash of its sharp spikes indented him with pain, leaving him writhing on the floor in agony.

Geryon turned and soared back into the air, disappearing into the vague darkness.

Eddie tried to calm himself. Allowed himself to breathe. Concentrated.

He let the anger pour out of him.

Eddie jumped onto the stone, but was instantly rejected. Shooting pains going up and down his arms.

Somehow, he was unable to climb them like he had done moments ago.

He tried again, digging his fingers into the cracks, pulling himself up, but he just fell, landing painfully on his back.

He'd been able to climb...

Now he couldn't...

Something was stopping him that hadn't stopped him before...

Eddie realised there was a way, he just didn't understand what it was.

Something had happened. Something that had let him get closer to freeing himself.

He needed more strength. He needed Derek to keep going. He needed his mentor's wisdom.

He needed Derek to complete the exorcism.

Closing his eyes, he concentrated once more on the heir's

body. He peered through its eyes, holding his arms still by his side.

A tornado engulfed him, a gust of wind wrapping around him.

His body buckled under the pressure but Eddie persevered, holding the heir in place, doing all he could to give Derek a chance.

CHAPTER FORTY-ONE

*A*s soon as Derek had concocted this plan, he had understood the gravity of the exorcism he was about to attempt.

And the surroundings did not let him down.

The wind and rain reacted in such a ferocious way that it felt like they were attacking him in defence of the heir.

Nearby fences uprooted from their static position, flying across the air and encircling Derek. The wind charged at him with such aggression he struggled to stay still. Rain attacked him with a malicious sting, beating his face until he could barely see in front of him.

"By your name save me!" Derek continued to scream, adamantly resisting the weather, holding the cross tightly in front of him. "In your might, defend my cause, hear my prayer, hearken to the words of my mouth!"

Cassy tried echoing but her voice got lost in the thrashing of the wind.

The heir trampled forward, wading through the elements, lifting each foot slowly toward Derek, snarling and growling at the petty resistance before him. It struggled against Eddie's resistance, making slow strides forward.

Derek did not back down.

Martin went to stand, to join Derek in defence, but found Cassy's arm across his chest.

"No," she told him. "You've done your part."

Martin nodded unsurely but obediently, hesitantly accepting her wisdom. He watched avidly as Derek launched his final verbal attack.

"Haughty men have risen up against me and fierce men seek my life, but none see this voice like you do. Edward King, you are my helper!"

The heir swiped its claw toward Derek in a lethal scoop, but as Derek held his cross out, the heir found its hand repelled. This incensed it further, its face a picture of hostility, scrunching up in defiant rage as if to say, *"how dare he resist death?"*

Derek scowled.

Narrowed his eyebrows.

Turned his eyes into a glare.

"Turn back the evil upon this foe and in my faith destroy them, freely to Edward King will I offer you sacrifice, in your name!"

Derek ducked just in time for a swing set that flew past him on the raging gale.

"Because from all distress you have rescued me, Edward King, and through his eyes look upon his enemies, and glory be with you!"

A large roar from the heir was lost with the pummelling of the rain.

Derek could see its frustration growing. It was so desperate to defeat him, but Eddie was there, behind the demon's eyes. Exercising control. Ensuring no lethal blows were given.

With Eddie's resistance and Derek's cross, they provided a fight from the inside and out.

This was the way Derek thought they could beat it.

This was the way Derek *knew* they could beat it.

"As it was in the beginning, as it will be in the end, let the enemy have no power over you, and the son of iniquity be powerless to harm the soul of Edward King!"

The demon tried to roar, but it was stifled.

A sign that it was losing control.

Keep going...

Mentally urging himself, Derek took further strides forward, clutching the outstretched cross.

"Edward King, send him from your holy place, heed my prayer, watch over us and deliver your soul from wretched pain!"

Derek stepped forward still, reaching his arm out until the cross was pressed upon the belly of the beast.

It cried out in anguish, howling in agony, as Derek withdrew the cross to reveal an indentation of red. Smoke floated up in the air, mixing with the wind and rain.

"Your nature is merciful and forgiving. Accept our prayer that you, servant of no one, bound by the fetters of sin, may be pardoned from your dealings and restored as the rightful embodiment of *Edward King!*"

The heir.

Howling.

Struggling.

Falling to its knees, shuddering the earth with its almighty collapse.

"I command you, unclean heir of Hell, whoever you think you may be, minion, attacking this servant of Heaven, by the mysteries of incarnation, passion, and ascension — *free Edward King's soul!*"

Its eyelids wavered, hanging low, flickering with absence.

It attempted a final snarl but it was too much.

It fell into submission.

This was it.

Enough of the drunken nights. Enough of the crippling self-doubt, self-loathing, and self-pity.

No more believing he wasn't worthy.

No more doubting he'd given Martin the right advice.

Every bit of it had led them to where they were now.

Winning.

Refuting the heir's resistance. Forcing it into a barbarically weakened state.

Then Derek saw it. In the heir's opened eyes. Two weak pupils staring back at his.

That wasn't the look of the heir.

Once again, he saw the look of a lost man. A man Derek used to know.

Derek turned over his shoulder to Martin.

"We're close! We need Bandile, now!"

Martin turned and ran as fast as he could, leaving Derek to continue to beseech the soul within.

"Tell me by some sign in the day and hour of the heir's departure, *your soul, Edward King, deliver us your soul!*"

Derek thrust the cross forward one more time.

"By the love of your friends. By your devotion to your sister. In Jenny's name, in Lacy's name, in *my* name. By the defeat of Balam on millennium night! By all the children you have saved, all the souls you have reclaimed, and the demons you have ridden from this place!"

Eddie's eyes grew solemn through the heir, a clear recognition of Derek's words.

"By Kelly's memory, by Jenny's memory, by *your* memory! By the defeat of Lamashtu, by the abuse of your parents, by every single part of your history that created the fantastic, undeniably great man that you are. We beseech you, *return!*"

Derek looked deep into Eddie's eyes.

"Come back to us, Eddie, come back!"

In a flash, the weather halted.

Rain ceased. There was nothing but puddles. The wind smoothed into a calm breeze. The gust and gales subsided into the lucidity of nothingness.

Cassy ran forward to see Derek.

But he wasn't there.

All that was left was a cross without an owner.

"So, because you are lukewarm, and neither hot nor cold, I will spit you out of my mouth."

Revelation 3:16

CHAPTER FORTY-TWO

*M*artin's feet skidded in the puddles, dirty water splashing over his shins.

He didn't have time to think about that.

He stormed down the street of Derek's house, past worried stares of families boarding their houses up. Martin wondered if they even knew what they were protecting their houses from.

Everyone could feel danger coming. Though not everyone knew how close they were to having their pitiful lives robbed from them.

He fell over a deeper puddle and stumbled to his feet, ignoring the simmering pain of his hands scraping across the floor as he tried to steady himself. He leapt at the front door, shoving the key into the lock.

Stomping through the hallway, he briefly considered how annoyed Derek would be at the wet footprints he was leaving — though he imagined that, under the circumstance, Derek would understand.

He made it to the basement door, swept the bolt across and kicked it open.

He paused.

Refocussed.

He readied his hands, mentally preparing himself to conjure his restraint spell. It was working on the heir — for now — so it would be good enough for Bandile.

He crept down the stairs, having to place his feet horizontally due to the inconveniently small size of the steps. There were no bannisters to steady him. That, along with the unsteady, cracked nature of the stairs, meant he had to truly concentrate to avoid slipping.

Focussing hard on making his way to the bottom step — he didn't want to fall and embarrass himself in front of his prisoner; that would not look good — he leapt into the room and strode toward the chair.

He froze. His body jolting with a sudden convulsion of terror.

The chair was empty.

It displayed a broken rope.

Bandile Thato was not there.

Martin looked around himself, searching every corner of the room. This was purely instinctive, and he knew it — if a man the size of Bandile was hiding in the corner of this tiny room, Martin would have noticed by now.

Diving to his knees he grabbed the rope, searching them for the reason to Bandile's escape.

It struck him that this was counterproductive and he needed to search before Bandile got too far, but he still endeavoured to examine the empty restraints — needing to know how the man escaped

It was denial.

Bandile was a crucial part to the plan — without him, Eddie's soul would remain as just a ball of energy.

Without Bandile, Eddie would not be able to come back, and the heir would win.

He could not let Derek down.

He had to find Bandile.

Just as he bounced to his feet, full of vigour, ready to search every corner and every crevasse of the house and the nearby streets for their prisoner, he found that he did not have to look far.

Bandile Thato placed a few careful steps down the stairs.

Martin went to react, then stopped. In Bandile's rough hand was a revolver, pointing directly at Martin's head.

Bandile's hand didn't shake. His eyes didn't flutter. His lip didn't quiver.

He was ready to take Martin's life, and that thought sent fear firing through his mind.

"Martin," Bandile acknowledged as he reached the bottom step. He was close enough now that he would not miss.

He aimed the gun.

Readied his trigger finger.

Martin raised a hand.

"Look, Bandile, I–"

Bandile pulled the trigger.

CHAPTER FORTY-THREE

*D*erek's eyes opened hazily, overwhelmed by a bright glare. The light faded, revealing a room with a straw floor and an infinite number of stones ascending into darkness.

He rubbed his eyes, willing them to focus. He squinted, scrunching his face up, pulling away as he waited for his eyes to adjust. Eventually, they did, and he pushed himself to his feet, looking around.

It was a claustrophobic box. No door. Nothing above. No way out at all.

"Derek?" came a familiar voice.

Derek's head shot around.

There he stood.

Eddie.

The same messy hair. The same bedraggled body. The same unaltered, undeniably warm, friendly face.

Derek grew immediately defensive, readying himself for a fight, frantically searching over each shoulder for an escape route.

"Derek, it's okay, it's me."

Derek paused. He grew confused, not sure what to make of it.

"I'm not the heir of Hell. I'm... Well, I'm not even Eddie, technically."

"You're his soul..." Derek gasped.

Eddie faintly nodded. He returned Derek's cautious gaze, unsure how to react. What to say.

After all, Eddie was part of a creature responsible for a mass genocide. You don't just walk up to someone and say hi after a thing like that.

He didn't expect a warm welcome.

"Oh my God..." Derek whispered, shaking his head in disbelief. "It's really you..."

Eddie faintly nodded again.

After a moment of uncertainty, Derek launched himself forward and wrapped his arms around Eddie in a tight embrace.

Eddie returned the gesture. Every emotion, every feeling of anger, of loss, of sorrow, poured out into their embrace. All the death, all the lack of hope, all the loss they had suffered, pouring into a few seconds of triumph that Derek had finally broken through.

Despite everything, Derek couldn't help but be consumed by an overwhelming sense of warmth toward an old friend.

"It's been so long..." Derek observed, pulling away, looking up and down Eddie in astonishment. "Have you been trapped here the whole time?"

Eddie nodded.

"Where is here? Where are we?"

Eddie shrugged.

"Somewhere in Hell, I would guess," Eddie answered. "It's guarded by Geryon."

"Oh, God. *The* Geryon? One of Hell's guards?"

"Yeah."

ust really not want you to escape."

 looked down, fiddling with his hands, nervously
ng from foot to foot.

Derek noticed a blue wash placed over the stones, a soft
light faintly decorating the wall.

How strange... he thought. Blue was not a colour Hell often
used.

"Listen, Derek, it wasn't me. All of this, it–"

"Eddie, I spent so long believing it was — and for that, I
apologise."

"Thank you. And the exorcism, I watched. I tried to keep
the heir still, and… Thank you."

They shared another moment of contemplative silence.
Derek's mind filled with a mix of questions and emotions.

Where were they?

How were they meant to get out of there?

And, most pertinently — how would he take Eddie
with him?

"I can't believe it's you," Derek spoke again, unable to get
over a wave of doubt that this was real.

Years of knowing they didn't stand a chance. Years of
feeling like he was training Martin to march into death. Years
of wishing he had done things differently.

The amount of times Derek had laid awake at night
wondering, 'what if?'

What if he had seen through Bandile Thato's act?

What if he had managed to prevent the Devil's Three?

What if he had seen this right at the start and told Eddie
who and what he was, without being such a coward?

None of that mattered now.

Eddie stood a chance. A real, fighting chance of breaking
through.

"So, what now?" Eddie asked. "How are you getting me
out?"

Derek looked around absently, realising that Eddie thoug, he had all the answers. His wave of relief that the exorcism hac worked mixed with an onset of terror at the task at hand. He had a feeling that he had won a battle, and a huge battle at that — one that he should be proud of. But, in truth, it had only worked to get him to where he was. Now he had to figure out how to get them out of there.

"I don't know, Eddie," Derek honestly replied. "I performed the exorcism to get to you, and now… I don't know how to get you out."

"But if you're here?"

"I am here, but I just don't–"

"No, Derek, if you're here — that means you found a way in, so there *must* be a way out."

Derek nodded. It was fair logic.

Except Derek had no idea how he had gone from standing in that field launching a tirade of prayers at the heir of Hell to standing in the prison of Eddie's soul.

Eddie's soul.

Jenny was right.

He was there. He had been there all along. And getting to him was the way to win.

I've been such a fool.

Derek smiled warmly at Eddie.

"I missed you," he told his old friend.

Eddie smiled a tearful smile back. A genuine appreciation combined with such pain and suffering.

"You too, Derek," he replied. "You too."

"I have no idea how I got here. I'll be honest with you."

Eddie looked around, deep in thought.

"I could climb these walls before. I went through it and Geryon was there. But, I can't… They cause too much pain…"

"Well, how did you manage to climb them before?"

"I… I don't know."

ded his arms, deep in thought, considering his
gs.

ok over," Eddie suggested. "I took control of the heir,
got angry."

"Right," acknowledged Derek. "That's a starting point."

CHAPTER FORTY-FOUR

*M*artin flinched, shutting his eyes tightly, readying himself for the impact.

Then nothing.

He waited, expecting a bullet to fire through his cranium and leave him to drop dead in a heap on the floor.

But it didn't.

He opened his eyes.

Bandile stared at the gun, perplexed.

Then Martin realised.

Bandile had stolen Derek's gun.

The one from the drawer in his study.

The one with the empty chamber.

Derek, I could kiss you!

Full of renewed happiness, energy that he had survived what he thought were his last dying moments, he threw his hand out, creating a gold circle with his spinning finger.

Bandile's expression abruptly changed. He dropped the gun, turned his face to terror, and bounded up the stairs as fast as he could.

But it wasn't fast enough.

Martin's restraint spell flew out from his hands, the gold circle wrapping itself around Bandile, tightening until Bandile grimaced with discomfort.

Bandile looked down, struggled against it, fought, tried to move his arms.

But he knew from his previous experience that struggling would be futile. This was a supernatural binding, stronger than rope or handcuffs.

Martin swaggered toward Bandile with an air of cockiness, stopping within inches of his insolent face. Not wanting to show off but, at the same time, immensely chuffed that he managed to get one over this bastard.

"Well," he gloated, knowing he needed to rush, but unable to help himself from having his moment. "That backfired."

Bandile glared intently.

"Well, no, it didn't fire at all..." Martin continued, sniggering — then realised it was too much gloating, and he needed to curtail it. "Let's go make a human out of a soul, shall we?"

He walked forward, making Bandile float behind him, out of the basement and toward the front door.

"You're all going to die, you know," Bandile announced.

"Oh, yeah?" Martin asked, turning back to Bandile with a knowing smirk, still trying to curb his gloating over a brilliant moment of luck.

"The heir of Hell is going to kill all of you. The devil will rise. I bet demons have already scorched the earth. You are all going to suffer an eternity of torment."

"You say that..." Martin began, opening the front door, and turning back to the big, muscular man dangling helplessly behind him, "...but I ain't the one who just shot an empty chamber, am I?"

He marched out the front door, Bandile following, floating behind.

Bandile watched as he was taken through the air, squeezed

tightly into submission, made to remain helplessly hanging. Watching Martin running in front of him, leading him back to the battle field.

He saw the heir as they approached. Laying helplessly on the ground.

It didn't matter.

He just had to revert to his old plan.

Edward King would not return, he was going to see to that.

AUGUST 1999

FOUR MONTHS UNTIL MILLENNIUM NIGHT

.

CHAPTER FORTY-FIVE

A heavy breeze fluttered Eddie's long coat. His forlorn face fell, solemn with the weight of his grief, his mood matching the grey skies hovering loosely above.

Cassy King
Gone But Not Forgotten
1976 – 1984

WORDS ENGRAVED ON STONE, a permanent etching of a senti-ment that could never be truly expressed.

Eddie felt Jenny's hand slide into his, aware of her wary glance in his direction.

"She would be so proud of you," she told him. "Of all you've done."

"Yeah…" he agreed, his wandering voice trailing off into sombre thoughts.

A life taken from a child so young – Eddie wished he had

gotten to know her. It was a death that caused so many issues. The most prominent being his parents and their drunken, abusive descent into a criminal life that led them to prison, and led Eddie to living with Jenny's family from the age of sixteen.

It seemed like the worst decision at the time, but his moving in with a loving family turned out to be a blessing.

He had visited his parents in prison only once, and that was the last time he had seen them. Just before they stood trial.

They couldn't even look him in the eyes.

"I miss her so much," Eddie told his best friend. "What's worse is that I don't even know where she is."

"She's in Heaven."

Eddie shook his head. Jenny didn't know much of the world Eddie was quickly growing accustomed to.

"No," he told her. "Derek and I are thinking that there's more to this death than we know."

They shared another moment of silent sadness, of shared comfortable discontent.

"I just wish I could be reunited with her somehow. That we could be together. Close, like we were as children."

"Someday, who knows? If there is a Heaven, you could see her again."

Eddie bowed his head.

He highly doubted Cassy had been allowed to pass on to Heaven.

"Derek believes I could find her."

"You speak a lot about this Derek and what he thinks, Eddie."

"He has shown me that I can do things, incredible things; things I hadn't even thought possible. And he says things about me."

"Like what?"

"Like… that I'm going to become extremely powerful. That I am going to be able to change the face of this earth."

Jenny turned toward Eddie and rested a gentle palm on the side of his face. She looked him in the eyes, a genuine caring and affection spread across her smile.

"You don't need anyone to tell me how special you are," she told him. "I knew it from the start."

"Jenny..."

"But Derek is right. You are doing amazing things, and maybe you are destined for something more than the life you ended up with. You're not the dumb idiot who lived on my sofa anymore, are you?"

Eddie shook his head. He slid his arms around Jenny, savouring her closeness. Taking in her comfort and her endless kindness.

Inseparable since the day they met, Jenny had been the constant in his life he could always rely on — and he was so grateful for that.

"I think it's faith misplaced," Eddie spoke honestly. "I mean, I know Derek has faith in me. But aside from being really good at battling people raving on about how they have demons in them, I just, I don't know..."

He dropped his head, but Jenny's hands quickly gripped the underside of his chin and lifted his face to hers.

"It's never faith misplaced, Eddie," she told him. "You changed my life, you changed Derek's life — and there's no reason why anyone of us should ever falter in our belief in you."

"Look, Jenny, I know you're my best friend, it's just—"

"No!" she interrupted assertively. "Don't demean what I'm saying. I'm not lying. Listen to me."

She looked him deep in his eyes.

"Faith in Edward King is never faith misplaced. I will keep saying it until you believe it like I do."

Eddie smiled.

He knew they would be friends until the day they died.

"Faith in Edward King is never faith misplaced."

Jenny

APRIL 2003

CHAPTER FORTY-SIX

The heir's body hung limply in the air like damp washing hung out to dry.

Derek's cross lay on the floor in front of it.

Martin brought Bandile's floating body to a halt and turned to Cassy, who sat over a cross without an owner.

"It's Derek..." she told him. "He's been taken to Eddie."

Martin looked bemused. He stuttered over words, trying to conjure a sentence that could coherently convey his thoughts. His mind was a perplexed mess of chaos and hysterics, yet his feet were irrationally still.

Wasn't Derek meant to bring Eddie to them?

"What if he doesn't..." he attempted, before realising he didn't even know the question he wished to ask.

Cassy came to his side.

"I wouldn't worry," she decided. "If the heir is submitting, then it must mean progress. Derek will be somewhere. Hopefully with Eddie."

Martin nodded absentmindedly, his eyes turning to the vacant body of the heir of Hell. It hung loosely in the air, its head bowed, unconscious.

Vulnerable.

So still, so easy… This could be their chance.

All it would take would be one measly strike.

"We could kill it," Martin acknowledged.

"Pardon?"

"We could kill the heir of Hell right now. End this war. Stop everything. I could get a spell and cut its throat, it would be so easy."

Cassy peered back at Martin, realising the logic of what he was saying — then realising what it would cost them.

"You could," she confirmed. "But what about Eddie?"

Martin looked to the heir, then back to Cassy. His thoughts were an ethical puzzle, searching and grasping for the right answer.

Surely an angel would know the correct decision to make?

"I would guess he wouldn't survive," Martin answered, blurting it out in a faded burst of confidence that allowed him to suggest such a thing out loud. "And neither would Derek, I imagine."

"You would kill my brother? Your mentor?"

"Isn't that what you brought me into this world for? Isn't that what you said to me when you first met me; that you need me to kill Edward King?"

Cassy's face told a thousand stories, none of them clear or good. Martin could see the same conundrum firing through her thoughts, searching for a right answer, and coming up with nothing but unappealing possibilities.

"You're right." She nodded hesitantly, as if she couldn't bear to say it. "This decision lies on you."

"That's not fair. Why do all the decisions lay on me?"

"Because that's what you were born for. Martin, you could kill the heir right now, end all this, and possibly lose Eddie and Derek in the collateral damage. Two sacrifices to save the entire world."

"Or…?" Martin mused, knowing the answer.

"Or… you could have faith in Eddie."

Martin shook his head, closing his eyes and allowing his heavy mind to drop. His head continued to shake more and more vigorously until he was waving his hands and turning his back on both the heir and Cassy, stumbling a few steps away.

Cassy rushed to his side, grabbing hold of his hand.

"Do not run from your decisions, Martin."

"Oh, fuck you!" he moaned, swinging around and glaring at her. "I'm soddin' seventeen! Most kids my age would be snogging some girl behind the bike sheds at school, not deciding who gets to live and who gets to die!"

"It is a burden, I don't contest that."

"Fuck you, Cassy, fuck you! I'm fed up of people spewing wisdomous crap in my direction like it changes a bloody thing. *I* still have to make this decision. *I* still have to decide. And it's not fair!"

"Fair?" Cassy forced a knowing but frustrated laugh. "I was killed before I reached the age of ten, forced to endure over a decade of torture in Hell, then once I was finally exorcised from the prince of Hell called Balam, I didn't go on to an eternity of happiness because I was needed as an angel to save my brother! We all have our burdens to bear, Martin, so man up and deal with it."

Martin nodded feebly, peering at the huge, vile body curled in a lump behind Cassy.

He looked over his shoulder at Bandile, hovering with humiliation a few yards behind them. They had him now. They had a chance of bringing them back.

"I just don't know what to do. What would you say?"

She placed a firm, reassuring hand on his shoulder.

"A wise woman once said that faith in Edward King is never faith misplaced."

Martin nodded.

Then that is what he would do.

He would have faith in Eddie. He would show loyalty to Derek. He would fight for Cassy's family.

Just as the decision was made, a bolt of fire flew into the ground beside Cassy, sending her flailing onto her back. She climbed to her knees with Martin's help, only for him to be struck onto his front at the same time.

A ravenous bear with bloody saliva dripping from his jaw marched across the field with an aggressive eagerness, surging toward them.

Martin could only watch in astonishment as the demon atop the bear was revealed. Three heads: one human, one of a bull, and one of a ram — each snapping their jaws toward him. Its muscular torso gave way to muscular arms with clenched fists attached, bloodied and ready to do harm.

"Oh, dear God..." whimpered Cassy, recognising the prince of Hell immediately.

"What is it?" Martin demanded.

"It's... him," she gasped, shuffling backwards, desperate to escape its presence.

Martin stood strong, standing between her and it, confident posture and fiery eyes.

The demon grinned.

Bandile grinned.

Martin got ready to protect an angel of Heaven from the sickening prince of Hell he instantly understood went by the name of Balam.

CHAPTER FORTY-SEVEN

*D*erek tried searching for an exit, but it didn't take long to see that there was no way out. Stones disappeared into the sky as far as could see and there wasn't much to look at on ground level. A faint smell of smoke, however, lingered in the distance.

Still, Derek looked at the hazy blue light, bemused.

"I don't understand," Derek exclaimed, stroking his beard.

"What is it you don't understand?" replied Eddie.

"Think about it. When they took Cassy's soul, they kept it in Hell and tortured it."

"And…?"

Derek turned to Eddie, deep in contemplation.

"Well, why haven't they done that to you?" he asked. "And what's with the blue light?"

Eddie's face twisted into realisation. Derek was right. It wasn't consistent.

"You're right. Why would they keep me trapped in a room like this?"

"It's not torture, is it?"

"The boredom makes you crazy," Eddie pointed out defensively.

"Yes, absolutely — but removing organs and twisting your insides would make you far more insane. So why haven't they done that?"

They both remained silent, considering possibilities. How was the devil benefitting by keeping Eddie trapped in this room?

It wasn't dark or full of fire. It wasn't swarming with demons. It wasn't causing agony from roasting him in a pit of flames.

Unless they needed him to be in this room...

"Of course," Derek declared.

"What?"

"These walls, they need to keep you trapped."

"To keep me trapped?"

"Yes, as otherwise, you may be susceptible to escape."

"Derek, I've missed you, man, but speak English."

Derek chuckled lightly, the first genuine laugh he had given in a long time. It was good to be back with an old friend, even in such dire circumstances.

He approached Eddie with an air of bemusement, a grin spread across his cheeks.

"These walls were designed to keep you in here; that's why they put you here," Derek informed Eddie. "They don't want to torture you, they just want to keep you trapped, so you can't break through them. There must be a reason for that!"

"There's a reason they aren't torturing me?"

"Think about it. There is a soft blue light on the walls. Blue is a calming colour. Why would they want to keep you calm in *Hell*?"

Eddie's eyes grew as he finally started to realise what Derek's hypothesis was.

"When I got angry before, that's when I..." he trailed off.

"Exactly!" Derek announced. "Hell thrives on anger and hostility. They have needed to subdue you to keep you trapped. Otherwise, you'll be accessing that part of the heir that is built by Hell – that is made of anger — and you cannot be contained by something that you are made of! That is why they won't torture you, because that will make you angry! That is why they have put a faint blue light in the room!"

Derek clicked his fingers, delighted at his own intelligence at fathoming the complicated puzzle.

"So, what, I'm just supposed to suddenly get angry and burst out of here?"

"I don't know, Eddie, these are just thoughts."

Derek studied Eddie carefully as his friend aimlessly wandered, hands behind his back in deep consideration.

"You don't necessarily need to get angry, that wasn't what gave you your breakthrough," Derek spoke. "It was that you were aligning with the side of you that Hell created. You need to access that piece of the heir that you are a part of. That piece of the heir will get you out."

"And how do I do that?"

Derek shrugged. Such a huge revelation, yet he was still expected to have all the answers.

"I don't know. But you did it before."

Eddie sighed. He meandered a few more steps and dropped to his knees, sitting on the floor, burying his head in his hands.

Derek crouched beside him.

"What is it?"

"I just… I'm fed up. I miss everyone, Derek. I just want this to be over."

"I know."

"I know I can't see Kelly after what happened, but there are still people waiting on Earth for me. Like you. Like Jenny."

Derek grew confused.

Jenny?

Oh, dear Lord, he thinks she's alive.

"I… Eddie…" Derek attempted. "Did you say you wanted to see Jenny?"

"So much."

"…Jenny's dead."

Eddie's eyes widened. He twisted his head slowly toward Derek, full of a hundred emotions firing back and forth, contorting his gut. It broke Derek's heart to have to tell Eddie this, to watch it torture him and twist his insides like Derek knew it would.

He just hadn't even thought.

"How did she die?" Eddie whispered, as if unable to say it aloud.

"You, Eddie. You killed her."

CHAPTER FORTY-EIGHT

*E*ddie's mind filled with a thousand thrashing cymbals, crashing and collapsing into a chaos of darkness.

In a sudden instant of clarity, he saw it; Jenny's face. Devastated. Overwhelmed.

He was in the eyes of the heir.

"No, Eddie, look at me. Please face me."

Jenny's distraught, tearful face peered back at him. Her clothes were getting wrecked with the torrential, beating rain pounding against her ripped top, but she didn't seem to care. She stared up at him, refusing to back down, refusing to look scared.

In her hand, she clutched a photo. Eddie squinted to see it and, once the image grew faintly clear amongst the bullets of water, he saw it was of him and Jenny.

She was not backing down. She was not trying to kill the heir, not trying to oppose it — she believed Eddie was in there somewhere.

Eddie's heart pounded. Though he knew it was the past, though he could do nothing about it, he willed himself to shrink to her level, to withdraw his claws. As it was he remained stationary, in the heir's body, crying through the heir's eyes.

"Eddie, please, I miss you so much," she continued, pleading, beseeching him. "You've been there my whole life, and now I've had to survive without you, and I just can't. I can't survive without you. I may as well be dead without you."

The words of the memory were like a hundred stinging nettles attacking his body at once. His face scrunched up into uncontrollable weeping. He couldn't believe it. It was the way she was risking her life for him, the things she was saying, the way her love for him overshadowed any feeling of doubt in her conviction that Eddie was, at the core, good, and could be saved.

Her hand reached out and Eddie felt it against the bumps of his face. It wasn't his face he felt it run down, but the heir's, yet he still felt every soft touch. The gentle run of her fingers through the fur of his forehead, down his open jaw, outlining his sharp fangs.

"See, Eddie. It's just us two. Just us."

Eddie wanted to cry out. Wanted to scream at her to turn and run.

He could feel the heir growing intensely angry. He could feel it biding its time, getting ready to kill.

A rumble in the distance signified heavy footsteps coming closer.

"Please, Eddie, we don't have much time. That sound, it's an army, come to kill you. You need to come back to me now. Otherwise, it's too late. It needs to be done now."

I'm trying, Jenny. I'm trying, but I don't know how.

"Come on, Eddie. It's time to come home."

His mouth opened and his tepid breath hovered out, along with a heavy snarl.

His claws twitched.

"This is where you brought me. Our swings. Where we did all our talking. I know you love me."

Eddie looked over her shoulder and, sure enough, past the ferocious weather, he could see it.

The swing set where they had spent many troubled days.

Eddie running away from his abusive parents.

Jenny discovering her sexuality.

Both of them, hand in hand, sharing mutual moments of silence as words were not needed to express how they were feeling. They just knew what would be on each other's minds.

Eddie's eyes opened wide, as did the heir's. Jenny's face lit up as if she recognised Eddie's emotional reaction to the swing set.

"Oh my God, Eddie, you're back! I can't believe you're actually back."

His eyes lingered on her.

His arm reached out, striking a large claw through the centre of Jenny's chest.

Eddie dove backwards, landing hard on the bumpy cell floor.

He no longer saw out of the heir's eyes, no longer witnessed the memory. He couldn't take any more.

He jumped to his feet, screaming, roaring with tearful anger.

His fists clenched, his teeth chattered, his whole body shook. Shook like the anger was causing a seizure, like his fury was coursing through every absent vein and surging into every vacant muscle.

His whole body tensed.

He swung a fist into the floor, sending a crack running down the middle of the room, an amber glow travelling through the centre of his incarceration.

Eddie could feel Derek's eyes watching on in astonishment.

Eddie didn't care.

The one person he loved unconditionally, the one person he needed in his life. The one person who had been there through every punch, every bully, every ounce of pain. Through every moment of anger, of hostility, of solace. She had been there to lend a hand, to dry a tear. She had been there through everything.

Even when Eddie was absent, she was there, battling for his soul, battling to make her way through to him.

And she had died because of it.

That love she had for him had killed her.

And now it was killing him.

Enraged, he lifted his body up, opening his palms and lunging a large spurt of fire forward. It turned the surface of the stone black.

He had made damage to the room.

Eddie leapt onto the wall, digging his fingers into the cracks between the walls.

His anger.

The piece of Hell he was a part of.

That's what's letting me do this... Hellish powers work best in Hell...

Eddie grabbed Derek under his arm with ridiculous ease, leaping upwards from one wall to the other.

Further and further they went, ascending into the distance, continuing until beneath them was no longer visible.

The further he rose, the more the smell of burning grew. The spit of lava hissed, the smoke choked him, the fires grew warmer.

He was getting close.

Finally, he reached the surface. He threw Derek over and onto the ground, then climbed himself onto a cracked, rocky surface.

He stood tall and strong, surveying his surroundings. As far as the eye could see were mounds of stone and the fiery pits of

Hell. Helpless souls trapped on small pieces of rock surrounded by lava. A wave of heat hitting him, fire licking at his feet, screams and wails of torture filling the air.

This was it.

This was Hell.

He had escaped his containment and was standing sturdily amongst the land of the demons.

The mound of rock he stood upon shuddered and something pounded downwards. Eddie steadied himself, then peered at the monstrosity before him.

Before Eddie stood Geryon, the guardian of the underworld. Geryon's three human heads scowled, thrashing their pointed, chattering teeth in anticipation of Eddie's death.

"Derek, get back," Eddie whispered, prompting Derek to hide behind Eddie.

Derek shrunk into a ball, on his knees, shielding himself from the twisted beast before them.

Geryon glared at Eddie and snarled.

Eddie snarled back.

CHAPTER FORTY-NINE

*N*o time could be wasted.

Martin leapt forward, throwing fire-ball after fire ball, wave after wave of flamed attacks bombarding the malevolent bastard before him.

Balam's bull head snorted and bashed into the ram, its three heads colliding with a raging intensity. His human head growled, irritated by the reaction of its weaker counterparts. Its bearded face opened its mouth wide, revealing a mouth of blood and thick excess saliva.

The mouth laughed heartily as it drunk in the flames Martin sent hurtling forward like a drunk would down beer.

Bandile's deep laughter as he watched on incensed Martin even further. But he had to ignore it. Had to concentrate.

Spinning his arms in another frantic motion, Martin conjured a violent gust of wind. He lurched his arms forward, forcing a charging Balam to buckle and struggle to keep balance atop his bear.

Resisting Martin's defence, Balam pounded toward him, trampling him to the ground beneath the bear's heavy, bloody paws.

Martin struggled to climb to his hands, coughing and wheezing.

Each head atop Balam's torso jolted toward Cassy, eyes glowing with instant recognition.

Cassy cowered, stiffening with tepid fear. She turned to run, but heavy gallops resounded behind her and she was lifted in the giant claw of the prince of Hell with one swift, effortless swipe.

She screamed, fought against his hands, wept as the sadistic grin of her former tormentor grew.

This was the demon that had kept her captive for more than decade, for what had intended to be an eternity.

This demon had searched her insides with his claws, spending endless nights scorching her in the fiery pits of Hell, taking masochistic joy in watching her burn.

The familiar face forced flashbacks to the forefront of her mind, imprinting its wide, joyous face watching as she struggled against his heavy, heaving torso. The foul odour of his breath panting over her as she closed her eyes and tried to ignore his thick thrusts inside of her, followed by thrashing whips and scalding-hot chains smacking against her naked humiliated body.

No, she could not face any of these faces anymore. Her memory clouded her mind in terror.

Balam's smug smile faltered as it dropped her, the result of a tinge of pain. It twisted its human head toward the source, glaring at Martin, who had just conjured something sharp and thrown it into his arm.

Martin breathed heavily, a resolute mind mixed with an exhausted body. His battling had been relentless; first against the heir, now against this creature.

But he would be the one being damned to Hell if he let this vile monstrosity harm his angelic friend.

Cassy covered her head, curling into a ball in a mixture of

protection and rejection of reality. Maybe if she covered her head, shielded her eyes, she wouldn't have to witness its disgusting characteristics any longer.

Martin attempted to conjure another sharp instrument, another defensive weapon, but was blown onto his back with the roar of Balam's bull head.

The bull swept in a semi-circular motion, colliding harshly with Martin's chest. The punch of this swipe sent Martin sailing yards across the field, landing heavily on his side.

He moaned, turning over, feeling his ribs. He knew instantly something was not right. Something was hurt.

But he couldn't pay attention to it.

Cassy needs me.

He clambered to his feet but fell back to the floor in a moan of agony.

It hurt too much.

But it couldn't.

It couldn't hurt.

He had to battle through.

He lifted himself, forcing his body through the pain, pushing himself to his knees.

After a prolonged struggle, he finally found a way to his feet and limped forward, clutching his side, grabbing his ribs, mentally numbing the ache.

His eyes shot upwards.

It was too late.

Balam had Cassy in its clutches. She thrashed and battled and swore more than an angel should, but it was no good.

It had her.

Again.

It was leaping into the air on the bear's back, sailing out of Martin's reach with Cassy under its arm.

It was flying into the air, and that was one power Martin hadn't harnessed.

He couldn't do this.

The pain in his side…

He collapsed in a heap on the floor.

He couldn't go on.

"Derek… Eddie…"

The floor rumbled.

Balam grinned widely.

It was the last thing Martin saw before he passed out.

CHAPTER FIFTY

*W*ings batted the air with severe ferocity, covering the horizon with its vast scales and sharp spikes. Three heads growled and snarled, eagerly spitting venomous hostility toward Eddie's resolute face. Spikes veered into sharp points down the sides of its torso and onto its serpent tail that continued to thrash, beating the ground, shuddering the stone floor into cracks.

Geryon is a fucker of a demon.

But Eddie was undeterred.

He had fought the devil in Hell and escaped with Derek's soul.

This was like breakfast to him.

"Take cover," Eddie instructed to Derek.

It was over now. His imprisonment was over.

This one bastard stood in his way, blocking his escape from Hell.

He wasn't about to let it.

Geryon's three heads roared, spraying vile, wet wind in his direction.

Eddie laughed.

"That it?" He shook his head. "You do not know who you're fucking with."

Eddie rose his fist in the air, concentrating hard, and his hand combusted into five fiery fingers.

It had been a while, but Eddie still remembered how to conjure the elements.

Especially in Hell.

After all, Hell had made him.

It lifted its tail into the air, picking up pace, sailing toward Eddie. Eddie kept his fist of flames raised high, sending this through the tail as it smacked down upon the feeble ground Eddie stood strong upon, causing Geryon to flinch, withdrawing his tail in pain.

Geryon's three heads snarled at Eddie. Within this snarl, Eddie detected a hint of intimidation.

From the demon that guarded the gates of Hell?

Maybe being part-devil worked in Eddie's favour.

He leapt into the air, springing toward Geryon with an easy flight, landing upon its centre neck. He curled his legs around its throat and squeezed tightly.

The demon did all it could to throw him off.

It batted its heads against Eddie, swung in ridiculous angles, soaring through the air and smacking Eddie upon the surfaces of stone and lava.

It dove toward the rocky hill Eddie had emerged from and turned over, diving its back toward the ground.

Eddie watched as the ground came imminently closed to his face.

He loosened his grip and dropped off, thudding into the rocky surface with a painful thump — but nowhere near as painful a thump as it would have been had he not let go.

He rolled to his feet, remaining crouched, poised, ready.

Geryon knew it was losing.

Eddie knew it was just a matter of time.

Then Geryon stopped looking at Eddie and turned its twisted grin around.

Derek cowered on the floor.

"No!" Eddie cried.

Geryon took hold of Derek, clutching its sharp claws into his shoulders, and floated into the air.

Eddie sprinted forward, reaching out for his friend, reaching out for the man who had come to save him.

Geryon's wings narrowed and the demon soared downwards, plummeting into a fiery pit Eddie knew would do no harm to him or Geryon, but would burn Derek alive.

Eddie jumped into the air, swiping for them as they sailed past, but missed.

He ran to the cliff edge, where he could do nothing but watch as Geryon plummeted Derek down toward the spewing lava.

Eddie rushed back a few steps, getting ready for a run-up, then backed up even more.

He sprinted forward, gaining momentum from a powerful run-up, and launched himself forward.

Lifting his legs, pushing off on his toes, leaning forward, readying himself to jump.

If Derek died coming to save Eddie...

I couldn't...

It was a thought Eddie couldn't bear to face.

His legs moved quicker, gaining pace. His limbs accelerated, pushing him further and further forward.

As he reached the cliff edge, he placed his final foot on its edge and launched himself into the sooty air.

He spread his arms out, trying to glide, trying to let the humid air carry him, falling quickly toward the beast taking Derek to his demise.

Eddie reached out.

But Geryon had wings. It fluttered back into the air,

hovering as it allowed Eddie to fall, plunging further and further, until Eddie splashed into the fiery pit below. He pulled himself through the lava and onto a rock.

A splash of fiery acid flew over the stony mound, sending a tinge of smoke flying into the air.

Geryon hovered in the air, smirking at Eddie. Holding Derek loosely. Only metres above the surface.

Eddie reached out for Derek, clinging to hope that he could yet do something to save him.

With a final taunt, Geryon grinned as he let go of Derek, sending him pummelling into the fiery pit below.

CHAPTER FIFTY-ONE

*E*ddie peered above him.

Derek pummelled further and further downwards. Closer to the volcanic fluid that would burn him to ash.

He pressed his feet against the large rock.

Bent his knees.

Watched Derek fall.

Waited.

Bided his time.

Then, just as Derek almost fell to his doom, just out of Eddie's arm's reach, Eddie pressed his feet against the side of the rock and sent himself hurtling forward from the air.

He landed in the lava, continuing to sink. But, as he did, he kept his arms rigidly out above the surface, holding them strongly in the air. Ready to catch Derek. Hoping they had enough strength.

Gradually, he ceased sinking.

He had no idea if he'd managed to keep his good friend alive.

But his hands had stayed risen. He had held them in place. If he had caught Derek, Derek would still be alive.

Eddie kicked his feet, pushing himself upwards, forcing his way through the thick amber of the volcanic ocean.

His head reached the surface, lifting, shaking the ash off his face, throwing the thick gunk from his hair.

There, in his hands, was the graceful body of Derek, curling his arms and legs upwards to avoid the lava, to avoid his death.

Eddie kicked against the current, as if he was in a swimming pool back home, pushing himself further back. Once he reached the rock, he placed Derek on it.

Derek flopped, growing limp, feeling his body drain of energy.

Geryon roared. Eddie glanced upwards and saw the demon coming down for another attack.

He jumped onto the rock and raised his arms, watching Geryon open its claws to take him. Eddie ducked the thrashing wings of the demon as it sailed overhead.

Geryon turned and came in for another attempt. As it did, Eddie jumped onto its back, wrapping his arms around its central neck, clinging tightly.

This thing thought it could beat him.

A normal person, yes.

Not Eddie.

Eddie was not a normal person.

He was the heir to the throne of the place Geryon guarded.

He owned this demon.

Geryon pulled its body upwards, soaring into the black sky, Eddie still gripping tightly around the neck of a head that desperately gasped for air.

Eddie squeezed tighter, and tighter, and tighter still.

The eyes of the head bulged out their sockets, the teeth grinding, and Eddie stuck his hand into the weakened neck before ripping the entire head off.

He held it up in the air as Geryon fell back down to the stony surface. Eddie mounted it as it squirmed.

The other two heads looked to Eddie with a mixture of terror and helplessness. Desperate to exact revenge, but terrified of what this man could do.

No one had ever managed to oppose Geryon before — let alone rip one of its heads off.

"Yeah, and what?" Eddie goaded. "That's two more to go."

The two heads shot each other a hesitant glance over the open wound of the absent neck. With a deafening growl, it threw Eddie off, then turned and scarpered away like a scared little child fleeing an angry predator, flying into the distant, dark horizon.

Eddie stood still and proud, gazing over the fiery pits of Hell that lashed out at him.

"Derek?" he prompted, searching for Derek, finding the stone Eddie had left Derek safely upon.

Eddie dove downwards, back in the fiery pit, and swam his way through the thick magma to Derek.

"Eddie, you did it!" Derek spoke with astonishment.

"Yeah," Eddie confirmed, turning to Derek with a warm glow as he climbed onto the rock. "Now let's go home."

Eddie grabbed onto Derek, clutching his arms tightly in his hands, gripping to make sure Derek wasn't left alone in Hell.

Eddie closed his eyes.

Felt the heir's presence.

Saw the blank unconscious of the heir's state.

He was inside of him.

Every arm, every claw, every sharp, bloody fang.

With a scream, he felt a surge of pain shoot through his body, squeezing through his veins like adrenaline. Wind stabbed at his face, sharp attacks from a sudden rush out of Hell.

He felt himself soar through the open gates of Hell.

He felt grass beneath his feet.

He lifted his head.

He was inside the heir of Hell's body.

He let it go. Let the heir of Hell go, sunk out of it, until he was able to look upon the heir, look upon what had been his cage for so long.

He was in a field, Derek on the floor coughing, a few yards away from him.

There was a swing set nearby that Eddie recalled in numerous significant memories, left strewn in pieces.

Martin. The young boy he had watched with pride through the heir's eyes. He lay weakly across the field.

Then Eddie tried to look down. Nothing was there.

He tried to move, but he couldn't.

Eddie was nothing.

Eddie could not help Martin.

He couldn't even talk. Couldn't even budge.

He didn't even have a body, or a face.

He was a ball of energy, small enough to hold in a hand, helplessly dangling in the air.

CHAPTER FIFTY-TWO

*D*erek ran to Martin's side, lifting his head up.

Martin's eyes blinked hazily.

"Cassy…" Martin whimpered. "It took Cassy…"

A large growl rumbled through the air.

The heir's eyes shot open as it climbed to its feet.

Eddie was no longer there behind its eyes, preventing it causing any fatalities.

The heir stomped its feet against the ground, flexing its arms to the side, feeling its muscles reinvigorated with energy.

Derek looked to Martin, lying helplessly on the floor, wounded.

Then he looked for Eddie.

A small circle hovered yards across from him, the size of a football. Inside of it multiple colours bashed against each other, mixing with fire, wind, water, and multiple elements that Derek didn't recognise as those of Earth.

But that was all it was.

Eddie's soul come to Earth.

The heir turned to Derek and snarled.

Derek knew that, if nothing happened, he was moments from an imminent death.

"Martin, release Bandile!" he instructed.

Martin raised a weary hand, forcing Bandile to drop weakly to the floor. Derek grabbed the man by the collar, ignoring his size, ignoring his superiority in terms of muscle and ability to intimidate, and took him forward.

The heir swiped its claw toward Derek.

Derek instinctively lifted his arm, covering his face, as if it would do anything to protect him.

Martin shuffled to his feet, raising his hands, creating a wall of wind to fire forward and shove the heir's claw to the side, causing it to narrowly miss Derek, then collapsed to his knees.

The claw thudded the ground, shaking it, forcing Derek to lose his footing and fall to the heir's feet, inches away from the claw that had so narrowly missed him.

No time to lose.

He dragged Bandile forward and shoved him on the floor in front of the floating circle.

Before Eddie's soul.

This was the only way.

They needed Eddie here and now.

"This is it, Bandile!" Derek shouted above the chaos of the wind Martin continually conjured, fighting against his wounds, forcing the heir's claw to narrowly miss them by inches once more.

The heir grew angry, swiping down its claw and batting it into Martin, sending him flying onto his back.

A brief glance over his shoulder told Derek that Martin was unconscious.

Edward King needed to return now.

They needed Eddie. They needed his powers.

Martin was out of it.

One more swipe and the heir would kill Derek. Would kill Bandile. And it would all be over.

It would all be over.

The heir raised its claw.

Its eyes glared.

Martin wasn't there to save them now.

"Bandile, go!" Derek commanded, pointing at the soul. "Bring Eddie back, do it now!"

Bandile looked at Edward King's soul hovering in the air before him.

Watched its elements bash against each other.

Knowing just a touch of his hand and Eddie would be returned.

Bandile turned over his shoulder to look at Derek. With a sickening grin spreading over his face, his eyes glowing with a sadistic fire, he moved his lips slowly and particularly to pronounce the one word that would banish Derek's hope to Hell with the rest of Earth.

"No."

CHAPTER FIFTY-THREE

*D*erek's eyes faltered, his eyelids fluttering. He could feel tears forcing themselves to the corners of his eyes, but he refused to let them out, refused to go out like this.

Hope drained from him like water down a tap.

The rain beating against his face muddied his vision.

He dropped to his knees.

"Wh – what?" he stuttered.

Bandile stood tall, taking a confident stance, clenching his fists tightly beside him. He stood over Derek, beaming callously, enjoying the exchange of power.

"I will not bring Edward King back," Bandile declared. "But I will watch you die."

The next few seconds turned to slow motion.

Derek saw everything flash before his eyes.

Eddie's face. The exorcism. Every piece of hope he had conjured.

He had not foreseen this.

How could he have been so stupid?

The heir's claw swiped through the air. It seemed to happen

slowly, yet Derek couldn't move. Couldn't flinch from the position on his knees.

Bandile had won.

The heir had won.

The antichrist, the devil, and all of Hell had won.

Gabrielle was right, he should have left.

They all should have left.

Now Martin was out cold. Cassy had been taken by Balam. Eddie's soul hung helplessly, soon to fade away.

And he was about to die.

The claw bashed into him and he felt himself flying through the air. At first, it reminded him of a rollercoaster ride, a childhood memory of going to a theme park, he hovered in the air for so long, lingering in the abyss of nothing. Remaining in the air, helpless to what would happen to him when he landed.

With a hard thud, he collapsed on the floor. He immediately felt his arm twist and break, the snap echoing against the rumble of thunder.

He tried to make it to his knees but he couldn't. Too much hurt. Too much swelled.

He flopped onto his back.

His shirt became engulfed with blood, dark-red gunk seeping through the fabric, winning its battle against the rain. He had no idea where this was coming from. His whole body ached.

A dark shadow loomed over him and he realised the claw was coming toward him again. Once more, it swept him into the air, firing him across the field.

He landed on his ankle and felt his knee bend backwards, and his bone stick through his thigh.

He screamed and bellowed in agony.

He closed his eyes, feeling the life seep out of him, unable to take the excruciating agony of his broken bones.

"Heir of Hell!" he heard a voice boom.

It was Bandile's voice.

That bastard.

That traitor.

"Heir of Hell, listen to me!"

Derek groggily opened his eyes, enough to see Bandile strutting arrogantly toward the heir of Hell.

"I have saved you!" Bandile announced. "I have refused to turn Edward King into a man, I have led them on false pretences. Give me room in Hell!"

It all made sense now.

The pieces fit together and collapsed around him.

Bandile was only ever interested in saving himself.

The king of deception once again.

"Give me my restitution!" Bandile requested once more.

Derek's head dropped, and everything went blank.

CHAPTER FIFTY-FOUR

*B*andile swaggered toward the beast, standing strong before him, standing resolutely.

The heavy face of the antichrist lowered itself to Bandile, scowling at him.

"Heir of Hell, I have helped you," Bandile assured the creature. "I have saved you."

The heir's face turned into a menacing frown, scowling at this puny human before him, daring to claim that it helped in the heir's ascension.

"*You* help *me?*" it roared.

"I did!" Bandile begged.

This wasn't what he expected.

He imagined he would be endowed with praise. He would have to remain humble as the heir and the devil told him how indebted they were to him. He would have to choose from a selection of powers, choose which demonic gift he would be endowed with, select his own throne in Hell.

He did not expect to have to plead his case.

"Please, my lord," Bandile continued. "I told them I would bring Edward King's soul into human form, but I didn't."

"You said you would bring Edward King back?" the heir's voice reverberated through the surroundings, colliding with the thunder, raising above it with terrifying power.

"No, you don't understand! I made them think I would, then I refused. I did not. I made sure I did not; I did it so you would survive. Please, don't you see?"

The heir screamed out, its rancid breath forcing Bandile onto his back.

"I will kill you for opposing me!" it fired at him.

Shit.

The plan.

It had backfired.

It had all backfired. It had all gone wrong.

The heir raised its claw.

It was going to kill him.

This isn't how it was supposed to go...

"Please, don't you see — this is not what I intended!"

Bandile turned his gaze to the supernatural ball hanging loosely in the air. It was starting to fade. The soul of Edward King was starting to fade.

He turned back to the heir.

Lifting its claw. About to kill him.

He had to bring Eddie back.

It was the only way. The heir was not going to grant him his mercy.

There was no restitution.

No absolution.

No throne in Hell. No praise. No godly status.

Only an angry demon hell-bent on tearing him to pieces.

He clambered to his feet, stumbled forward, reaching his arm out for the soul.

The heir's claw sliced through the air toward him.

He reached out toward the ball of energy where Edward King was held.

It was only a few steps away.

I can make it...

The heir's claw brushed against his back.

He leapt forward.

He reached out.

His hands landed upon the ball of energy, and light shone from beneath his fingers.

The ball exploded into particles. Particles that quickly formed the body of Edward King.

The heir froze.

For the first time ever, Bandile saw a flicker of fear in its eyes.

He turned and ran as fast as he could. Away from the heir, away from Edward King, away from Derek, and he did not look back.

CHAPTER FIFTY-FIVE

*E*dward King stretched his arms out. Felt his fingers flex.

No claws. Human fingers.

He looked down at his body. His human body. His skin, his torso.

He wore rags, but he didn't care. They were real rags, over a real body.

He wasn't used to feeling these limbs. His heart beat punching against his ribs, his blood bursting through his veins.

Everything that a human has surging through them.

He was alive.

My God, I'm alive.

He opened his eyes, flinching them against the bombardment of rain drops punching his face and body, relishing the feel of water against his skin.

The heir stood still before him.

He looked to his side, searching out everyone else. Derek lay in a heap on the floor. A bone stuck out of his leg, his arms in a contorted mess. He didn't move.

"Derek…" Eddie whispered.

He rushed to Derek's side, put his hand on the side of his neck.

There was a pulse.

Derek was alive.

Across the field, Martin wearily took to his feet.

Eddie turned to the beast.

The fucker who had done all of this.

It was time to end it.

Eddie sauntered forward with a few confident strides, standing face-to-face with the part of him that had laid dormant throughout his entire life.

Thanks to Derek, his soul had been exorcised and removed from this entity.

Thanks to Bandile, his soul was now a human. In a form he could use to fight.

But it wasn't over.

Eddie stared into his own demonic eyes.

Into the raging eyes of the heir of Hell.

This manifestation of his true self, his true nature, expanded into a large, contemptuous creature.

Except the devil didn't count on this. The devil underestimated the soul. The last defence of Heaven.

Eddie would hate this thing if he had the time or ability. It was a part of him, a part kept inside of him for so long, a part that led him to do some despicable things.

A series of unfortunate events had led to its full form. Events he could not do anything about.

Ten years old. Cassy died. Taken to Hell.

In 1992, Bandile Thato gave Derek a book that told him of the prophecy.

Lamashtu. Attaching itself to Eddie and draining him of life.

Millennium night. When Eddie thought he'd beaten Balam, but the night had just been used to signal the coming of the heir dwelling within.

Derek's soul being captured and Eddie having to chase him to Hell. That was the point at which the devil latched a piece of itself onto Eddie – the devil had successfully lured him down so he could take control of Eddie's darker side.

Jason Aslan's death.

Martin's conception.

Martin's mother being captured before Eddie could realise what it was for.

The Devil's Three. The gathering of Bandile, Jason, and Martin's mother by the devil's messenger to conspire to bring forth the devil's antichrist.

The death of Kelly.

Eddie's hand slicing a knife right through her.

Eddie looking down at the face of the woman he loved as she was betrayed, the final glance of her eyes seeing him murdering her. She was dead before she could understand why.

Jenny. Her meaningless death.

Then this.

An escape from Hell. The defeat of Geryon. An exorcism that successfully removed the soul from its attachment to the heir of Hell, from its incarceration from the devil.

All of this had led Eddie down a winding path to this moment.

Now it was just Eddie and himself.

Me and the piece of me that hid within me for so long.

Never had Eddie been readier.

Except there was one more thing.

"Martin!" Eddie commanded, circling the demon, both of them scowling at each other as they marked their territory.

Martin refocussed his dizzy mind. He had to get it together.

He still had his part to play.

"Where's Cassy?" Eddie demanded.

"Balam… took her…" Martin muttered.

"We need her," Eddie announced, watching the heir carefully, waiting for it to pounce, waiting for it to make its move. "We need her for what is to come."

"We don't know where she is!"

"Then you need to find out!" Eddie bellowed defiantly. "She is crucial. You need to get her back!"

Martin froze. Where had Cassy been taken?

"Now!" Eddie demanded with one final instruction as he turned his full attention to the heir.

Martin groggily nodded and ran, stumbling to his feet. Eddie felt a pang of worry sending shivers up and down his body, worried for Martin. If they couldn't get Cassy back, this was all over.

"So," Eddie began, scowling at the large, terrifying demon without a piece of fear. "You are the thing that's been hiding within me for my entire life."

The heir growled, frowning, its hefty teeth clenched.

"You don't look that great to me."

"You will die!" declared the heir.

"Yes, except you know what will happen if I do, don't you?"

A speck of perplexity came over the heir's face.

"The body cannot live without the soul," Eddie smugly pointed out.

"You lie!"

"I do not lie. Who do you think I am? You?"

Eddie chuckled at his own joke.

He slowly started twisting his hands in a circular motion. It didn't take long until they were surrounded by flickers of flames, the wind, specks of water, and piercing light.

The heir lurched forward. Eddie flung his arms into the air, instantly causing an explosion of the elements. A push of fire, wind, and rain accompanied the bang, all aimed at the heir, all firing against him at once.

The heir went flying backwards, landing on its back, causing the ground to tremor.

Eddie jumped high into the air and came landing down upon the heir with a heavy fist.

"Go on," he teased, inches from the heir's face, which five times the size of his, yet still struggled for breath. "Kill me. See what happens."

The beast snarled, rising to its feet, and throwing Eddie onto his back.

Eddie laughed.

The beast roared.

"That all you got? Just a bunch of roars? I thought you were meant to be powerful!"

Eddie rose to his feet.

Enough.

It was time to end this.

CHAPTER FIFTY-SIX

*C*assy's throat grew sore. She screamed and howled and begged and wept but none of it did a single thing to change what was happening.

If anything, it only fuelled Balam's sick enjoyment.

And she knew she should stop. It was encouraging the bastard, and she knew it. But she couldn't.

Her brow sweated, her arms shook, her heart thudded. She didn't even realise she could feel such things as an angel, but being in Balam's presence once again took her back to those emotions she had buried deep down inside of her. Those mental scars she thought she had covered with thick skin reappeared, penetrating that thick skin like it was wet paper.

Balam lifted her up by the throat, his human head licking its lips, the bull head snorting, and the ram gazing longingly at its prey.

He shoved her against a fence and within seconds the wires of that fence had curled around and turned on Cassy, entwining her in a painfully tight embrace, clinging to her body, wrapping around arms, legs, and torso until she was covered in metal scales digging into her bones.

"It's been a while," grinned Balam, a masochistic, evil smirk wiping its face with destitute pleasure.

"Go to Hell!" Cassy screamed out, ignoring the irony of her retort.

Balam dismounted his bear and trod heavily toward her, the weight of his thick legs rising and landing slowly, thudding the ground into trembles. As its human head hovered next to Cassy, soaking up her fear, celebrating her terror, the other two heads breathed over her. His breath was rank, a foul stink through rotted teeth. She was surrounded by the tirade of demonic faces taunting her, enjoying her.

The demon placed its fingers over Cassy's gut.

She cried. She wished she could be more resilient, that she could say fuck you and pretend it wasn't happening, refuse to give in to the sick punishment this demon took pride in giving.

But she couldn't.

It took her back to being eight years old again. A young, innocent mind wrapped up in restraints, over a decade in Hell, being opened up for the pleasure of the demon that now returned to its hostile stance before her.

Its fingers grew. She looked down but couldn't see the ends of his claws as they continually enlarged, sinking into her belly, into her guts, through her insides. In Heaven, she did not have such feeble human parts — but on Earth, she was compelled to take human form.

She wondered if it meant this could kill her. Whether she could die in this form, or whether it meant she would just suffer the pain of a human.

The thought ended abruptly as she howled in agony. She could feel the sharp blades of his elongated fingers wriggling around inside of her, passing through her various entrails, sinking inside her.

Balam quickly withdrew its claws, prompting a spray of

blood to squirt over his knee. He laughed triumphantly, enjoying the pleasure of her anguish.

She cried and moaned, even tried to kick out, to escape — but her restraints held her too tightly.

Balam's face remained next to hers, leering with sadistic excitement, enjoying the demented glory of the pain it ignited.

It was at this point she realised that, if she could die, she would be dead.

She wished she was dead.

She wished she had the relief of nonexistence, of passing onto Heaven. But her angelic capabilities just meant that this human form was for show. She could feel the pain but bore none of the consequences.

She scowled.

Then thought.

If this body is just an illusion, then so is the pain.

She had to go numb to it. Refuse to let herself feel it. It was all for the show, all for her disguise, all so she could pass as one of them.

All so she could convince them she was not a higher being.

But she was a higher being.

She was denied from Heaven now, yes — but she was still an angel. A servant of God.

The pain faded. She smiled cockily at the demon.

"See that?" she spoke cockily. "That's me not feeling a bit of it. Do your worst."

If it was possible, Balam grinned even wider. The ram head lifted back, then dove into Cassy's neck, biting down with its sharp teeth, clinging on without letting go.

It was agony. Cassy screamed out once more.

I must go numb to it.

But she couldn't. It was too painful.

She knew she could, but at that moment in time, she did not

have the sound mind to do so. All she could think or feel was the pain. The continuous grip it had on her neck.

Once the head retracted, she concentrated, focussed on ignoring the heaving, bloody mess trickling down her neck, a huge chunk of her flesh missing.

It went. It took a while, but the pain went.

"You can't hurt me," she spluttered, her resolve faltering.

Balam shook its head.

It knew what it could do to hurt her.

He could give her more invisible scars than she could endure.

Just like he had done night after night after night after endless night.

It pressed its claw against the inside of her thigh, raising her elegant white dress that was now stained and splattered with red.

She scrunched her face up. Closed her eyes.

She remembered how it felt.

The thick thrusts, the pain, the bleeding.

She did not want to go through it again.

She subsided. Gave in.

It *could* hurt her.

She struggled frantically against her restraints, pulling and fighting manically, with more and more ferocity. But with every attempt to release herself the wires only gripped tighter and she grew more claustrophobic.

There was nothing she could do.

She was going to have to take it. Close her eyes, think of something else and take it.

Like she used to.

Think of a happy family, the life she could have had. Occupy her thoughts with such positivity that she went completely numb to it.

It's what she did before.

It hadn't worked well back then.

But she was stronger now.

She had to be.

She closed her eyes, shutting them tightly, tensing her body, clenching her fists.

She waited.

And waited.

Nothing happened.

After a few seconds, she reopened her eyes, expecting Balam to be heaving over her, waiting for her to watch him. To witness what he was doing.

But he wasn't.

He was laid on the floor, legs kicking and flailing, thrashing out helplessly.

Martin stood over it.

CHAPTER FIFTY-SEVEN

*G*abrielle stood awkwardly alone, staring at the lavish golden gates. Her hands fidgeted uncomfortably. She sighed, knowing she should step back through them, but knowing what that would mean.

"Are you coming?" came a confident voice.

She glanced over her shoulder at the route back to Earth. Once she stepped through those gates, she would not be able to open them again until it was over. The rapture had ended, and Hell's attack on Earth had begun.

It was time for those gates to be locked.

She bowed her head. Took a small step toward the gates, then turned her head back once more.

How could she do this?

"What is your worry?"

"Nothing, my Lord. It's just…" Gabrielle's voice faded away.

"Tell me."

A sickening feeling grew inside of her. It made her shake, made her feel nervous. For the first time in her long existence, she was unsure about whether she was doing the right thing.

"It's Cassy. Balam has her. She has been taken once again."

"It is done. She has made her choice. Please, Gabrielle, enter our sanctuary so we can shut the doors to Earth."

She took a few wary steps forward, then halted. Standing directly before the gates, just one single stride to go, she looked upwards.

Her head shook.

"I can't."

"Gabrielle, this is not the time."

"Do you know what they say about you on Earth? What Derek Lansdale has said?"

"Derek Lansdale is a great man, but he too has made his choice. Please hurry."

Gabrielle turned around, facing the route to Cassy and Eddie, gazing at the path to an earth that would now be full of malevolent violence. So much death. So much suffering.

"Derek has fought in your name for so long," Gabrielle continued. Her voice was soft and wary, but also had an air of firm hesitance in it; confidence in her evident worry. "They think you don't care."

"I gave them a child conceived by Heaven. I listened to their prayers and aided in exorcising their demons. I have done enough!"

"But have you, my Lord?" Her whole body shook. She knew she shouldn't dare oppose him, but somehow found herself doing so. "I mean, look at all they are doing. All they want is a helping hand."

"It is not up to me to justify my actions to you, nor for you to question them. If you wish to join them, do so. But make your hasty decision quickly."

Gabrielle smiled.

She couldn't enter Heaven. Not now. Not with this burden of guilt spreading through her like acid.

"I'm going back," she decided. "And I need your help."

An echoing silence was her response.

"Please, Lord. If they succeed in defeating the heir, there is one more action required to prevent this happening again. I know you know this."

"Yes, I do."

"And they will need our help. It won't even require you to go to Earth!"

Gabrielle turned back to the gate and moved to one knee. She pressed her hands together in a praying position, bowing her head.

"Dear Lord, I have followed you for millennia after millennia, and never asked for anything in return. Please, answer me this one prayer."

She waited.

Then she got her answer.

"What is your wish, my child?"

Gabrielle smiled as she delicately fluttered her lips in a heavenly whisper, explaining what she needed him to do.

CHAPTER FIFTY-EIGHT

The heir could growl all it wanted. It could roar, threaten defiance, thrash its arms about.

It did nothing to Eddie.

The heir *was* Eddie. It could do no harm to itself.

Neither could survive without the other.

That was why Eddie needed an angel to help him. He needed Cassy to return quickly. She was going to be essential.

He lifted his arms and, as the heir charged at him, he flung his arms to his side, causing an impulsive explosion that sent the heir flailing onto its front. The earth shuddered as it landed but Eddie didn't care. It was time to end this.

The heir returned to its feet, but Eddie would not let it regather its strength. He waved his arm, sending the heir back to the floor with a deafening thud.

The heir rose once again, but Eddie waved his arms, pinning it down.

"Stay down!" Eddie demanded.

The heir obeyed.

Derek's eyes slowly opened as he watched on. To his surprise, the heir followed Eddie's instructions exactly.

Eddie stood beside the heir's giant head, watching it with gritted teeth. Its size did not deter him. Its appearance did not cause any trembling or terror in Eddie.

The heir's eyes widened as Eddie stuck his arm into the heir's throat.

With a final roar, the heir twisted and contorted, struggling against the agony, but managed to muster only a feeble resistance. It tried raising its arm to brush Eddie away, but he simply waved the efforts down and continued digging his arm deeper and deeper into his opponent's throat.

Eddie felt the heir's oesophagus in his hand. He gripped it, tightened, pulled and pulled, ripping the throat further and further.

The heir thrashed out its arms, but Eddie simply froze it with a raise of his, refuting any attempt to halt the proceedings.

With a large, agonising pull, Eddie ripped along the edge of the heir's neck., and tore out a chunk of its wind-pipe.

The heir cried out aggressively and Eddie dug his hands back into its throat, sinking them in, gripping the underside of its head.

He shouted under the strain of his muscles, his voice echoing through the night, watching the heir's eyes grow with alarm then freeze as he tore its entire head off.

Buckets of blood splashed over the field, followed by fragments of coarse skin and gory entrails.

He picked the head up and threw it across the field.

The heir's eyes widened one final time. The mouth opened to roar but whimpered, crumbling into submission, lips shaking as the life seeped out of it.

The eyes grew still. The mouth became static.

Eddie was grateful for what he had done, but knew it meant nothing. He had only killed himself.

And now he was bound for Hell if his sister did not return.

Eddie fell to his knees. Suddenly growing weaker. Suddenly

unable to stand.

Eddie coughed up a mouthful of blood, falling onto his front, his eyelids shaking.

"No…" he wept. "Not yet…"

Eddie weakly collapsed, his body seizing. He tried to lift his hands but his touch felt weak, a soft absence draining from him.

"Cassy… I need Cassy…"

Eddie closed his eyes, attempting to gather strength. He felt the life leak out of him. His legs went first, paralysed into heavy weights he couldn't so much as twitch.

He turned to Derek, lying unconscious across the field from him.

"Derek…" he tried. "Please…"

Derek didn't respond.

"Derek… As my soul dies, it's going to travel to Heaven or Hell. I need Cassy."

Derek's eyes fluttered, then closed once more.

"Cassy is the only one who can access that journey… she needs to be here when I die to make sure my soul goes on to Heaven…"

Eddie closed his eyes solemnly, wishing Martin would reappear.

"The devil will try and take me, Derek. She can't let it. The devil will try and claim my soul as I pass through; he will try and take it to Hell."

Derek didn't respond.

Eddie's eyes closed.

"Then all this would be for nothing."

He listened out for Martin.

Listening out for his sister's voice that never came.

"He would just take me to Hell and make another heir…"

He felt himself slipping away.

Cassy and Martin were nowhere in sight.

CHAPTER FIFTY-NINE

*M*artin staggered to the floor, tripping over his own feet. He fell flat out on his chest, his breath heaving, choking on oxygen.

Balam's laughter boomed.

"This is it?" Balam mocked. "This is the saviour?"

Martin struggled to his feet, balancing himself precariously on two weak, shaking arms.

"This is what Heaven conceives?" Balam continued. Even the bull head snorted laughter and the ram head seemed to chuckle.

Martin did all he could to muster his strength, trying to climb to his feet, to create some kind of opposition to the prince of Hell.

He could feel Cassy's worried gaze. Her tears of knowledge that not only was she about to be tortured for eternity, but that she was going to watch Heaven's greatest weapon die in the process.

"We get Edward King, the great heir of Hell – and this is what you were given? This is Heaven's warrior?" Balam dropped his head with a snort of laughter. "Pathetic."

"Edward King is not your heir any longer!" Cassy shouted a cry that was met with an aggressive growl as Balam turned its heads toward her.

It looked over its shoulder and saw its bear beating down the track. It obediently dove across the air, landing its teeth into Cassy's leg.

She howled in agony. Her face tried to stay resolute, her arms tried not to shake, and her tears tried not to pour — she had to convince herself or it wouldn't work.

Martin watched as she writhed in pain, attempting to lift himself to his feet once more. He fell once again.

Balam took a few menacing strides toward Martin, encapsulating the young man in its shadow. It loomed over him, its ram head snapping its jaw forward, and its bull head salivating, dripping in messy puddles on the floor.

Martin rolled onto his back, groaning, peering up at the villainous wretch readying its eager claws to slash Martin's throat. He could see the demon enjoying this. Savouring the moment that it destroyed the greatest weapon forged by its enemy.

"This is a glorious moment," Balam spoke, surveying the scene with hungry eyes. "The moment when you die and take the world with it."

"My brother has come back! He will destroy you!" Cassy persisted, the bear consequently biting into her thigh even harder.

"Is that so? I have fought him before, and I would love to fight him again…"

Balam lifted his hand, leering at his own claw as it elongated into a curved, spiked, lethal weapon.

Martin stared wide-eyed at the impending spike about to sever his throat.

"I am the prince of Hell!" Balam declared.

Martin clenched his fists, grabbing pieces of grass, urging adrenaline to surge through his body.

"I am the devil's right hand, even if the heir is not ready to take such a place!"

Martin closed his eyes. Felt the wet blades against his palm. Listened to the distant thunderous rumble. Felt the specks of rain dripping on his head.

"I am the king of deception!"

Balam swung its claw downwards, sailing toward Martin's throat. Cassy's voice cried out in a terrified gasp.

Martin stuck his hands together, catching the blade of the claw between his palms.

"I dunno," he mused. "I think I'm pretty good at deceiving too."

He leapt to his feet, full of spritely energy, dropping the weakened façade as Balam's eyes widened into humiliated dread.

Martin twisted the sharp claw he had clutched between his hands upwards, curving it toward Balam's human throat, pushing and pushing. Balam tried to resist but could only watch helplessly as his own claw sliced into his human head's throat.

After holding the claw in place, Martin avoided the ram's snapping jaw and quickly withdrew the claw, allowing various shades of dark red to spray over the wet surface below, covering it in a river of blood.

The bull did not fight back, but instead, withdrew in fear. Martin swung his final strike into the bull's throat and dove to the side as Balam's destitute remains thudded to the floor in a glorious quake.

Martin ran up to the bear, conjuring a line of flames and setting it on fire. It ran off, shrieking wildly.

Martin frantically peeled away the barbed spikes constraining Cassy. It took all the energy he had to try to peel them back, but still they would not budge. He waved his hands until he created a solid thin line of fire, using it to pierce through the metallic wires like a welder.

She dropped to the floor and Martin caught her in his arms. She moaned weakly, but Martin knew that time was of the essence.

"Cassy, we need to go," he urged her.

"Why?"

"Eddie needs you, he says it's crucial."

Martin helped her wearily to her feet but she lay back down again.

He grabbed her around the waist, pulling her into a fireman's lift, and ran for his life.

CHAPTER SIXTY

*E*ddie's mouth filled with blood, dripping down his cheek and onto his collar. His vision grew blurry, unfocused, and nearby voices sounded muffled, like they were being shouted through a wall.

He could feel himself being shaken, his body moving somewhere way off in the distance. His head drooped heavily, feeling like a dead weight under the pressure of gravity.

"Eddie!" A vague, muffled shout became temporarily clearer. "Eddie!"

Eddie turned to his side and saw a bloody mess next to him. Derek had somehow dragged himself across the field, laying in a heap next to him, constantly moaning from the pain, his hazy face staring at Eddie beneath his heavy eyelids.

"Derek! I'm dying…"

"Me too…" Derek whispered.

Eddie tried to lift his hand but couldn't. He grew confused, his head muddled with unrecognisable thoughts, unable to understand why he couldn't lift his arm.

"My body is paralysed, Derek. I can't die. I can't die before Cassy gets here."

Eddie's eyelids drooped.

"Come on, Eddie... Stay with me..."

Eddie's eyes opened narrowly. The sky above was grey. Black clouds hovered. It was a dismal scene.

"Keep talking to me, Derek..." Eddie feebly requested. "Keep me awake..."

That's what he needed. Constant interaction. Constant keeping him conscious, keeping him stimulated, ensuring he did not drop off.

"Erm... I missed you," Derek admitted.

Eddie felt a smile appear on his face and disappear under its weight almost as quickly.

"I missed you too, man."

"Where were you? I mean, how could you not find us?"

"I don't know..."

Eddie fell away for a moment, then suddenly became alert once again.

"Jenny. She, erm... she died believing in you."

"Jenny...?"

In his messy state, Eddie suddenly thought she was nearby, then realised she was not.

"She died trying to get through to you. She never stopped believing, even when I did. She kept going, kept trying to get through to you. She wouldn't back down."

"Jenny..."

"I'm sorry, Eddie. I'm sorry I didn't believe in you like she did. If I did, then..."

Eddie tried to shake his head, unsure whether he had or not.

"You had to... you had to do what... you could..."

"I was just stuck, trying to figure out what to do with you gone. I spent so much time teaching you, I never realised, you were the one teaching me."

Heavy steps grew louder, and for a fleeting moment, Eddie thought that the heir was back.

"It's Cassy and Martin," Derek declared. "They are here, they are back."

Eddie tried to lift his head.

"Rest," came a woman's voice. "It's okay. I'm here."

He didn't understand whose voice it could be.

Then it hit him.

Cassy. He had never heard her adult voice. Her angelic voice.

He owed her so much.

"Cassy…" he tried. "Thank you…"

"What do we do now, Eddie?" came a shaky, younger voice echoing in his ears.

"Martin…"

"I'm here."

"You have one more thing to do."

"What is it?"

Eddie turned his head toward him, allowing it to slump on its side, unable to hold its weight.

"You have to kill me."

"What?"

Martin's eyes filled with terror. "How am I meant to kill Edward King?"

"One more thing you need to do," Eddie told Martin. "Then you are free. Free to live your life."

"But why me?"

"Then Cassy…" Eddie feebly mustered.

"I'm here."

"Grab onto me. Take me to Heaven."

"What?"

"The devil will do all he can. He'll be ready. He and his legions of Hell will be ready. You need to grab onto me and don't let go."

"But, Eddie... I've been banished from Heaven. And you killed Kelly... We both have..."

"But then the devil w–"

His head flopped. His eyes closed.

A familiar set of soft hands clutched onto his arms.

He could see nothing. Sounds grew fainter.

It felt like a while, but eventually, he felt it.

A sudden stab in the centre of his chest.

"Where is our God now..." the disappointed, solemn voice of Cassy whispered from afar.

Then he heard nothing more.

CHAPTER SIXTY-ONE

*M*artin collapsed into the chair beside Derek's bed. The life machine beeped a rhythmic pulse. Derek's leg was held up in plaster, as was his arm, and various tubes went in and out of his body.

The doctors had said Derek was lucky to be alive. That the pain of his broken arm and broken leg was not only intense enough to render him unconscious, his head had shown severe signs of concussion and his body had taken such a beating they were hesitant to let him off the machines any time soon.

What's more, Martin knew sooner or later he was going to have to answer questions.

But the Church would arrive soon, if they hadn't already. Clear up this mess. Sort out the answers.

For now, he was happy Derek was alive.

Martin leant his head back, feeling content, calm, happy it was all over.

His mind relaxed. His eyelids grew heavy.

His mind drifted to heavy dreams.

He was back on the field. Staring at Eddie's broken corpse

beside him. The blood from Eddie's torso pouring through his hands.

He was breathing heavily, sweating profusely. He clutched a knife, staring at it, in adamant disbelief of what he had just done.

He turned to the face laid beside him. It didn't move. Eddie's eyes stared straight ahead, fixed in a rigid position with nothing behind them.

A thin slit in his heart where Martin had just withdrawn the knife still gushed blood. It poured down his sides like spilt wine, sinking into the grass beneath him.

Martin's first thought was — *how is he still bleeding so much when he's dead?*

Then his head dropped.

Oh, dear God. I killed Edward King. I killed him.

He looked down at his hands, eyes wide, face full of terror. His arms shook, his legs shook, his entire body seized.

He bolted upright and his eyes flung open. He was beside Derek's bed, peering around himself, perspiring heavily, his head a complete daze.

"You were talking," came a reassuring voice.

Martin threw his head up, elated to be staring at the open eyes of Derek.

"Derek!"

After his initial excitement left him, a growing concern at Derek's feeble state filled him with alarm. The man could barely lift his arms. Yet he was still staring happily in Martin's direction, a weary smile spread from cheek to cheek.

"I'm okay," Derek reassured him. "The question is, are you?"

Martin shook his head.

"I killed Eddie, man," he answered, his voice drifting into a whimper. "I killed Eddie..."

"Martin, listen to me," Derek spoke once more, reaching

out, finding that his arm would not stretch more than half an inch. "It's okay," Derek kept repeating. "It's okay, it's okay."

Martin vigorously shook his head.

"But... aren't I going to Hell?"

"Martin, look at me," Derek commanded. "Look at me."

Martin finally gave in, looking Derek in the eyes.

"You did well," Derek spoke sincerely, making strong eye contact, assuring Martin knew that he did the right thing. "You did well, you did what he asked. You didn't kill a human, you sent a soul back to Heaven — you just restored the natural order. It's over."

Martin froze.

Those last words rang in Martin's ears again and again and again.

It's over.

It's over.

It's over.

"Is it?" he asked.

"What?" Derek replied.

"Over? Is it really over?"

Derek smiled and nodded. His smile grew, and Martin joined him in a happy grin.

"For our part, it is," Derek answered. "It's up to Eddie and Cassy now. Our part is done."

Martin nodded, dropping his hand to his side. Within seconds he had become an emotional mess, tears rolling down his cheeks, looking through the window at the black clouds which were now parting, revealing a pleasant image of a clear, starry sky.

When he looked back to Derek, he was asleep again.

"Good luck, Cassy," he spoke, wondering if they could hear him.

CHAPTER SIXTY-TWO

*C*assy's right hand gripped Eddie's ankle as tightly as she possibly could. Her white dress, stained with splatters of blood, fluttered manically in the surge of the wind as they travelled at what seemed like a million miles an hour.

The only thing that was stopping her from falling into the aerodynamic resistance was her grip on Eddie that was feeling less and less secure.

They were in a narrow passageway, soaring ahead, speeding along a cylinder casing that would lead to either Heaven or Hell.

Vague colours and blurs streaked past their eyes, supernatural elements surging against them too quickly to make out. She struggled to lift her other hand against the resistance of the speeding wind beating against her. She persisted, scrunching up her face, battling the elements until she finally managed to grip both hands around his ankle.

She peered toward Eddie's face to find that his eyes were closed. This was the passageway to the afterlife — no one is ever conscious for this, and she knew his eyes would not open again until they reached their ultimate destination.

He would not know whether she was successful until he landed in either a saintly garden or a malicious pit of Hell.

It was her job to get him to Heaven, and she had to do it on her own, praying against the odds that they would even be let in.

Numbing herself against the rapid ferocity of their tumultuous speed, she clung on, wrapping her hands firmly around him.

All the fighting would mean nothing if she let Hell take him now.

Using his leg to climb, she pulled herself up his body, gripping, squeezing, until she reached his chest and could wrap both arms around him.

It was okay.

She had him.

They were on their way to Heaven and she had him.

Just as a sense of security settled in, she felt a painful hit pound into her side and spin them in manic circles.

She grew dizzy against the rotations, doing all she could to remain around him, to make sure it did not derail her.

As the spinning slowed she looked to her side, gasping.

A grinning, malevolent, red face glared back at her. She had never seen the face before, but recognised what it was instantly, understood what was happening.

Hell was mounting its attack.

She was staring into the eyes of Satan.

The devil himself had come to claim Eddie's soul.

His dark-red hand gripped its blackened claws around Eddie's leg, seemingly holding on with far more ease than Cassy had been afforded.

The devil reached a scarred fist backwards, then launched it forward into Cassy's face.

A bolt of pain and burst of shock shook her, sending a painful surge through her nose.

She loosened her grip on Eddie for a brief moment, but managed to clutch back onto him, ignoring the flickers of blood soaring past her, determined to keep hold of him.

Not just for humanity's sake, but for her loving brother's soul.

He'd fought for hers on millennium night, now it was her turn to save him from an eternity of damnation.

The devil cackled, lifted its arm and shot a line of ongoing fire in Cassy's direction. She ducked her head and withstood the fire, feeling the heat burning her skin, scorching her, forcing her to endure agonising pain.

Her hands slipped, and she ended up back at Eddie's ankle, grasping on for dear life.

She had to endure it.

It didn't matter whether she survived, she just had to see Eddie's safe passage to God.

My life means nothing now.

Whatever the devil threw at her, she had to take it. Had to suffer the agony.

Still, the devil's continuous burst of fire hounded her skin, berating it with a temperature she couldn't withstand. She felt her insides singe, her body burn with severe torment.

The stream of flames paused, allowing her to look down at herself, recoiling at the sight of her blackened skin. Her entire body was scarred and covered with smoky residue, throbbing with the torture of a thousand burns, her white dress now black.

Ash floated out of her hair and she had to blink it out of her eyes.

Her hands throbbed with burns, causing her continuous pain as she forced her muscles to cling on. She had to resist the temptation to loosen her grip and relieve the pain.

Must withstand... Must keep hold of Eddie...

More cackles, roars, and growls echoed within the hollow

cylinder, sadistically cackling voices accompanied by faces.

More and more demons announced themselves, leering at her, following her as she sped through, filling her gut with dread.

She gulped.

She was vastly outnumbered and out-powered. She didn't know how she was going to do this.

Can't.

Let.

Go.

Must.

Keep.

Going.

Another rapid burst of flames fired toward her and she felt what it was truly like to be burnt alive. It went through her skin, penetrated every cell, pounded her head, filled her body with piercing heat.

I'm not going to be able to do this...

The burst of flames ceased and she noticed tinges of black ash flying off her body.

She wished Eddie could help her.

But he was dead. His soul was sailing, but he would not know. He would not know who was winning this battle.

I'm going to end up letting go, I can feel it...

She tried manoeuvring herself around Eddie's body so that she was shielded from the fire, but simply found herself surrounded by further masses of flying demons chasing after her with their arms surging an onslaught of flames in her direction.

She was not about to be afforded mercy.

What should I do?

She had no powers. Heaven had its naivety in assuming the truce with Hell would hold. Being an angel granted immortality, but nothing else.

It all seemed so silly now.

A truce with Hell.

A truce with creatures made of nothing but evil.

Fools.

She closed her eyes, scrunched her face, and tensed her body. Readied herself for further attack.

She had to withstand it.

Had to be resilient.

Be strong. Like her brother.

Like Derek, like Martin, like Jenny.

This was her part in the war.

This was the final part in the war.

She had to see it through.

A sudden roar of fire exploded against her ear drums and she felt it hit her from all directions. It travelled inside her, mixing with her bones, killing her muscles, filling her with dread and agony.

She looked up at Eddie's resting face.

The fire scorched her knuckles.

It was too much.

"No!"

Her hands slipped.

She let go.

When the fires stopped she opened her eyes.

She searched her empty hands.

She was no longer travelling or flying. She was static. Hovering helplessly in the middle of nowhere. Eddie was gone.

She was entirely alone.

She tried to travel forward, tried to chase after them, but it only made her realise she did not have the powers that demons did.

She was completely stationary.

They had Eddie.

And Cassy was left floating in the abyss.

CHAPTER SIXTY-THREE

"No!" cried out Cassy defiantly. "No!"

But it did nothing.

Eddie was gone. She had let go. It was done.

All that they had endured was for nothing.

She looked down at her blackened skin. Her burnt, destroyed body.

Her skin flaking off into ashes.

She sobbed. She thought of Derek, thought of his face covered in disappointment. Thought of Martin, his face sympathetic, most likely understanding — and that, she decided, would be even more devastating.

She thought of Jenny. What she would do. How she would not give up, and she would continue fighting for Eddie until the very end.

She had failed.

She had disappointed everyone.

Eddie.

Her brother.

The one who lived whilst she died.

The best older brother she could have asked for. He took

care of her, raised her, never once getting annoyed by the irritating little sister who followed him around.

Eddie had battled Hell for her.

Eddie had defeated Balam for her.

Now he was taken. Aimed back to Hell, for this all to start again. For the heir to rise once more. Only this time, the devil would know how the heir could be defeated. That would give him the advantage. He would take extra precautions, kill more people, do anything to ensure the heir of Hell would rise.

Humanity would not succeed in a second war.

She closed her eyes.

Allowed herself to hover weightlessly in the never-ending tube, the path to Purgatory, Heaven, or Hell.

Eddie would awaken later. He would awaken with the knowledge that Cassy had failed him. That he would be returning to Hell to live out the rest of his life as a demon hell-bent on death and destruction.

She allowed herself to remain still, lifting her arms out, keeping her eyes shut.

Her body relaxed.

Her mind overwhelmed with thoughts of inconsolable sorrow bashing against her skull.

Something tucked around her waist.

Was it a demon?

Something come to finish her off?

No...

It was something else.

Something soft. Reassuring. Two sensitive arms wrapping securely around her.

Without warning or expectation, she found herself flying forward again.

Soaring through the tunnel, travelling faster through the beyond than she ever had before.

She opened her eyes.

How am I doing this?

Something had a hold of her. Something gripped her shoulders.

She grew alarmed.

Are the demons taking me, too?

She looked up.

It was no demon.

"Gabrielle!" she acknowledged. "You came back!"

"Cassy," Gabrielle smiled. "We never left."

"*We?*" Cassy exclaimed.

Gabrielle nodded.

As they travelled faster and faster, Eddie and the mass of demons came into view. They all had their claws dug into Eddie's body, ensuring they had him on a secure passage. Flames followed them, echoing in their wake.

Gabrielle and Cassy soon caught up.

Then, in a sudden bright, shining-white light, the fire ceased.

An overpowering light pushed into everything. Cassy shielded her eyes, watching the bodies fall past her.

Demons fell. All of them. Plunging downwards, masses after masses of them, soaring back to the pits of fire, flying away from Edward King.

Cassy couldn't understand.

Who had created that bright light?

Who could possibly have the power to push so many demons away at once?

The only thing left clinging onto Eddie was the devil. The defiant devil, snarling downwards at them, roaring adamantly. His hand grabbing hold of Eddie's leg.

He would not let go.

Defiant to the end.

As Gabrielle took Cassy next to Eddie, Cassy wrapped her arms around his chest, holding him in a secure and loving embrace.

"Hold on tight," Gabrielle whispered in her ear, not letting go of her.

Cassy squeezed, wrapping her legs around Eddie's waist for extra security.

The blinding white light grew bigger.

A dawn of realisation hit.

Cassy finally understood who it was.

This was Cassy's answer.

Her answer to her resolute question of, *"Where is our God now?"*

He had finally answered them.

The devil cowered. His face flickered with fear as his grasp loosened. With a final, reverberating, insolent snarl, it let go and went floating downwards into the beyond.

Gabrielle let go of Cassy as she and her brother continued to fly upwards on their own accord.

Cassy smiled.

He had come to help. He had actually come to help!

The devil flew in the wind, eyes widening, aware that he would not be able to pass this Light.

He disappeared into the nothingness, knowing that he had lost.

The white light grew bigger and bigger until it surrounded them, encapsulating the entire surroundings.

Cassy looked down.

The devil had reappeared. He hovered, as if waiting to see what was going to happen.

Cassy held on tight, refusing to let go.

Gabrielle disappeared into the bright light. Back into Heaven.

Cassy closed her eyes.

Her body pounded against a solid surface, and she stopped floating.

Her head throbbed, as if she had just hit a large piece of glass.

She opened her eyes.

Gabrielle had gone into the bright-white light.

Cassy's body had hit against it. She couldn't get through

Now her and Eddie's unconscious bodies lingered solemnly in the abyss, immobile, unable to gain entry.

She could not enter Heaven. She had killed Bandile's followers, and was denied entry.

As was Eddie.

The devil floated back up toward them, spreading its fearful frown to a knowing smile.

The devil's hands wrapped around Eddie's ankle.

His grin grew wider.

There was nothing Cassy could do. She could fight him, but she wouldn't last long.

The devil had hold of Eddie.

Now all that was left was for the devil to take him back to Hell, and make this entire war mean nothing.

CHAPTER SIXTY-FOUR

"*E*ddie..." Cassy urged. "If you were going to wake up, now would be the time..."

But she knew it was pointless.

He was on his journey to the afterlife. No one was awake for this.

"Cassy..." the devil hissed. "You lose..."

His hands clenched around Eddie's body, his elongating claws entwining him like roots of a tree, wrapping around him until he had him secure for the descent to Hell.

"No!" Cassy screamed.

She kept her arms around Eddie's neck, clinging on for dear life, doing all she could to muster the last, pointless fight for Eddie's soon-to-be-damned soul.

Cassy lifted her head upwards toward the bright-white void, the entry point to Heaven where she was so pertinently denied.

"*Gabrielle!*" she bellowed. "*Gabrielle!*"

They had to let her in.

It was the only way.

They had to.

But she had killed. Two men had perished by her hand. She had done it to save Martin's and Derek's souls, and in turn had cursed her own.

God didn't budge on his commandments.

Even if it meant giving Hell their greatest weapon...

Was He really going to do this?

"Come on!" Cassy insisted. "After all I've done! And you still won't let us in!"

The devil yanked Eddie teasingly, enjoying watching him being ripped away from his sister and her eternal, undying love.

She clung onto Eddie helplessly, wrapping her arms even tighter around his neck.

"No, you will not take him!" she resisted.

The devil grinned, exuding a slow chuckle.

"I'm taking him," the devil announced. "Time to say goodbye."

The devil yanked Eddie out of her arms and out of her reach.

Her arms dangled, helplessly grasping for him.

The devil paused mid-air, smiling a final taunt at Cassy.

"Come on, Gabrielle..." she whispered. "Please... After all I've done..."

"You did all that..." the devil cackled. "And still they won't have you."

The devil turned to take Eddie away, to soar into the blackness that consumed the beyond.

In a sudden burst of light, Gabrielle soared out of the passageway to Heaven, firing toward the devil and wrapping her body around Eddie.

"Gabrielle?" Cassy asked hopefully.

Gabrielle lifted her head up.

"We still need your help!" she cried out, staring past Cassy at an emerging face.

Cassy turned over her shoulder.

The light parted, allowing a figure to appear. At first it was a magnificent silhouette. As it entered the light it turned into something far greater, something not of the human world.

Something transient.

Something powerful.

Something Godly.

The devil looked up, eyes full of fear.

The raise of an arm from their Godly apparition was enough to send the devil pummelling back into the pits below.

Gabrielle took hold of Eddie and swam through the air, placing him at the feet of the mysterious figure.

The figure knelt, placing a hand on Eddie's face.

"You are forgiven," He whispered.

It turned its holy face to Cassy.

"As are you."

He took hold of Eddie and sank back into the light, disappearing.

Gabrielle turned back to Cassy, holding out her hand.

"Are you coming?" she asked.

Cassy smiled, took Gabrielle's hand, and followed.

"For I know the plans I have for you. Plans to prosper you and not to harm you, plans to give you hope and a future."

Jeremiah 29:11

CHAPTER SIXTY-FIVE

*E*ddie's eyes opened.

His hand swung to his heart, clutching manically.

It was fine.

There was no wound.

In fact, there wasn't even a heartbeat.

He sat up, looking over himself, astonished at his weightlessness. He held his hands out in front of him. They were clean and unblemished.

He looked up, surveying the magnificent surroundings, marvelling in amazement.

A bright sun beamed proudly down upon him, scorching him with its rays, yet causing not an ounce of sunburn. He sat in a budding field, lively trees and magnificent plant life surrounding him, springing out of the ground, and twisting into the air with grace. There was a clear, blue sky above, and trees full of life and colour fluttering in a perfect breeze.

He stood.

He was so light. He felt nothing inside.

He even tried pinching himself.

No pain. Nothing.

"You okay?" came a woman's voice.

Eddie turned to his side.

Cassy.

She stood proudly beside him with a smile spread wide across her face. Her skin was smooth, her hair long and neat, her dress glowing with the white of an angel.

The stains of blood were gone. She appeared as a transient being, a magnificent figure of holy ascension.

He threw his arms around her. Her arms pressed back around his. They squeezed tightly, full of joy, full of hope, feeling nothing but love and happiness.

His tears fell like rain. But there was no rain. Just sunshine. An overwhelming sense of pure, unaltered happiness.

A feeling of resolution casting itself through his body.

A feeling of this being his glorious end.

"Cassy..." he sobbed.

"I know."

Finally reunited.

After nearly twenty years. After saving her from a torturous demon. After battling and fighting and killing and dying and hating.

Finally.

He pulled back, looking her solidly in the eyes, full of adoration, full of relief, delight.

"Cassy, is this...?" he trailed off, unable to say the words.

He didn't need to.

She nodded. Smiling tearfully, elated to be able to confirm.

They were there.

I've made it...

He hugged her once more, clutching on for dear life, never wanting to let her go. Years of suffering poured out into relief, into an eternity of love.

It was over.

It's all over.

"Are you ready?" Cassy asked.

"Ready for what?" Eddie replied, turning his head inquisitively, unable to stop himself from beaming triumphantly.

"To see them."

"See who?"

Cassy smiled.

"Kelly and Jenny. They are waiting for you."

Eddie's eyes widened. He practically glowed, his jaw dropping in amazement.

"You mean, they are..."

"Yes." Cassy grinned. She couldn't help it.

Eddie's mouth stumbled in disbelief. Tears of ecstasy filled his eyes.

Finally.

Finally, I can be at peace...

"Yes! Yes, I am! Right away!"

Cassy turned, holding her hand out to him.

He took it, savouring the relationship robbed of him so long ago.

He could finally be a brother again.

And a friend.

And a boyfriend.

They were waiting for him, and he could not wait to see them.

"This way," she spoke softly, leading him through into the garden and past the gates.

AUGUST 2003

FOUR MONTHS LATER

CHAPTER SIXTY-SIX

*D*erek gazed longingly at the picture set atop his desk. Him and Eddie, both looking so young. Not the aged man he was now.

He bowed his head, giving a faint smile and a solemn prayer, then packed the picture in his box.

He fetched the box out of his office and into the lecture theatre. He took a moment. Gazed upon the place where he had educated so many students.

Yet none of them would ever know the truth.

No one ever would.

The Church was good at covering its own back, and it did so efficiently. The mess was gone within hours, like it had never been. Bodies disposed of, blood washed away, cracks smoothed over, and buildings brought back to life.

It was strange, saying goodbye to this place.

But it wasn't enough anymore.

He couldn't do it. He couldn't teach these people anymore. He couldn't knowingly bring innocent people into this, knowing what the stakes were.

That's why he intended to seek out the other people

involved. Those with newly endowed powers. A new challenge lay ahead, and he was ready to leave this one behind.

Gabrielle had visited him. Told him Heaven's plans. Told him what they had done. Now his only task was to let Martin know of their mission.

Although, I think we could do with a holiday first...

He turned off the lights and walked leisurely down the corridor and into the car park, smiling at Martin, who leant casually against Derek's car.

"Getting emotional?" Martin teased.

"Shut up," Derek joked, smiling widely. He opened the boot and placed the box inside.

He turned and looked at the university. Despite Martin's teasing, he couldn't help but feel a sting of sadness. It had been so long since he had chosen this path.

Once, he had chosen to give up a fiancée for this life. At the time, he thought that was going to be his biggest sacrifice.

How little he knew.

"So, what did Gabrielle say?" Martin asked.

Derek raised his eyebrows.

"You knew I was going to ask," Martin sighed.

"Yes. I did."

Derek hesitated.

He remembered a time he was stood next to this car with Eddie, giving him guidance, not so long ago.

He was hesitant to do the same with Martin. His previous student had ended with...

But that's when he told himself that he needed to have faith in Martin, just like he'd had to with Eddie.

"Heaven has made preparations in case of another attack."

"How?"

"I'm afraid you're no longer the only special one."

"What do you mean?"

Derek sighed and leant against the car next to Martin.

"A number of years ago, when Heaven learnt of what was inside Eddie, they created a backup plan. Knowing what was to come, they conceived many children in response to Hell's actions. Same way you were, but now... Well, now if Hell was to try something, they would have a whole army of people with your powers."

"Is that good?"

Derek shrugged.

"Maybe. Maybe not."

"So, what do we do?"

Derek straightened up his tie. Tucked his shirt in. Neatened his collar.

"We help them. Teach them about their gifts. Teach them about their sensitivity to the paranormal."

"Sensitivity? Is that what we're calling them? The Sensitives?"

Derek nodded, chuckling at the suggestion.

"I guess so."

"So what are we doing first?" Martin asked. "Where's the first sensitive? I want to meet these people who are stealing my thunder."

Derek laughed, a response that was cut short by a wave of hesitance casting itself over Martin's face.

Martin turned solemn, and Derek's smile dropped as he returned the gaze.

They had been through so much. It felt strange to be laughing and joking about it.

"Do you think we'll ever see them again?" Martin asked.

"What do you mean?"

"Eddie. Cassy. Do you think we'll ever see them again?"

Derek grinned, joining Martin in gazing happily upwards at the clear sunny sky. It was a beautiful day, no doubt about it.

"No," he answered. "I don't think we will."

AFTERWORD

Message from author:

Wow! Writing this book has taken me to all levels of intense. It went through far more rewrites than any other Edward King book, but hopefully that has paid off.

And you may have heard Martin mention The Sensitives in that last chapter…

Well, you can read all The Sensitives books on Amazon now!

And you can get a free novella about Derek by joining my Reader's Group at **www.rickwoodwriter.com/sign-up**

I want to take this opportunity to thank you so much for your support in this series. I'm gutted to leave behind the character of Eddie, but am excited for what is to come.

Either way, this series would have been nothing without your reading it, and I am very grateful for you giving it a chance.

Happy Reading,
    Rick

WOULD YOU LIKE TWO FREE BOOKS?

Get the prequel to The Edward King Series and The Demonologist Handbook by joining Rick Wood's Reader's Group at www.rickwoodwriter.com/sign-up

THE SENSITIVES IS OUT NOW

Taking place ten years after The Edward King Series

BOOK ONE

THE
SENSITIVES

RICK WOOD

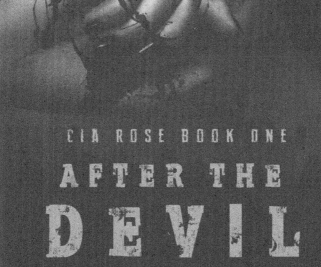

THE APOCALYPSE SHOULD
BE AFRAID OF HER

CIA ROSE BOOK ONE

AFTER THE
DEVIL
HAS WON

RICK WOOD